An Earl Unmasked

Ladies of Risk, Book 1

Rachel Ann Smith

Text by Rachel Ann Smith
Cover by Wicked Smart Designs

Dragonblade Publishing, Inc. is an imprint of Kathryn Le Veque Novels, Inc.
P.O. Box 7968
La Verne CA 91750
ceo@dragonbladepublishing.com

Produced in the United States of America

First Edition January 2022
Print Edition

ARE YOU SIGNED UP FOR DRAGONBLADE'S BLOG?

You'll get the latest news and information on exclusive giveaways, exclusive excerpts, coming releases, sales, free books, cover reveals and more.

Check out our complete list of authors, too!

No spam, no junk. That's a promise!

Sign Up Here

www.dragonbladepublishing.com

Dearest Reader;

Thank you for your support of a small press. At Dragonblade Publishing, we strive to bring you the highest quality Historical Romance from some of the best authors in the business. Without your support, there is no 'us', so we sincerely hope you adore these stories and find some new favorite authors along the way.

Happy Reading!

CEO, Dragonblade Publishing

PROLOGUE

Chestwick Hall

THE CANDLELIGHT FLICKERED and specks of forest green paint caught Lady Diana Malbury's eye. "Either the painter you commissioned for this portrait dipped their brush into the wrong color or your heir has rather unusual colored eyes."

The silver-haired Earl of Chestwick chuckled. "Nothing strange about Randal's eyes. They are simply hazel."

"Hazel?" Diana rolled to the balls of her feet and peered closer at the man's eyes in the painting, "Hmm…medium to light shades of brown, multiple variations of green, and…is that specks of gold?" She blinked twice to clear her vision. Intriguing. Definitely, no one of her acquaintance had such unique coloring. Her friends and family all possessed either blue or brown eyes of various shades; however, they easily fell into one of the two categories.

"Aye, well mayhap Mr. Graystone emphasized the yellow shards in the boy's irises a tad."

Diana's brows creased at the earl's remark. Artists were commissioned to paint their subjects with accuracy to provide future generations a glimpse into the past, not elaborate or embellish a person's features. Shifting her focus to the image of the younger man in the painting, Diana noted the strong familial similarities between the two strapping lads in the portrait. Both men had their papa's square jaw and defined brow line.

"Your younger son appears to have dark brown eyes." She turned to face her host and squinted. "Like you."

"The late Countess Chestwick was a beauty. Golden tresses with sky-blue eyes."

She tapped the toe of her foot as she studied Randal's image once more. Thinking out loud, Diana mumbled, "How is it that the future Earl of Chestwick, inherited neither brown nor blue eyes? Instead, Randal's eyes contain an arresting blend of warm forest colors that even includes rays of sunshine." It was a good thing none of her siblings were present while she had uttered such a poetic description. They would have certainly laughed at her choice of adjectives, and no doubt provided some long-winded, scientific explanation for their neighbor's eye coloring.

With no clear memory of the boy she had only occasionally caught a glimpse of from a distance, Diana examined the man in the portrait. Symmetrical facial features were scientifically proven to appeal to the majority; combined with the man's unique eye coloring, Diana was captivated by Randal's image. It wouldn't be a hardship to gaze into those eyes, ball after ball, or across the supper table. She shook her head slightly. Now was not the time for fanciful fantasies. Randal Wilson, heir to the earldom, the man destined to own her dream residence, was not likely to pay her any attention during the upcoming Season when she was to make her debut into society.

The gold flecks of paint reflected in the light, capturing Diana's attention. "Hmm. I believe I shall need to research the matter more."

"Grand. However, Randal has chosen to go and fight in the war. It could be years before..."

She interrupted the earl, "Oh, not the matter of your son. The science behind our heredity." Ready to view the next portrait along the walls, Diana stepped around the Earl of Chestwick, who she left staring at the images of his two sons.

Meandering down the long hall, Diana studied the various portraits. She mentally took notes, observing the high frequency of the Chestwick square jawline appearing throughout the generations. Diana paused in front of a painting of a woman that could be no other than the late Countess of Chestwick. The earl had described his wife in detail with much love and devotion in his tone that Diana believed Randal was the product of a love match. A rare occurrence amongst their set.

Staring up at the lady in the painting, words like genteel and poised entered Diana's mind. Neither of which Diana had managed to master, despite her mama's best efforts. Instead, Diana was often caught sprawled upon a rug in front of a fireplace with a volume full of poetry or a tome full of philosophic theorems laid out before her. It was her thirst for knowledge and access to such works that had led Diana to boldly introduce herself to the earl. The earl. Where had he disappeared to? "My lord?"

The old man's deep voice echoed down the hall. "In the study, my dear."

How long had she been dawdling in front of the fine reproductions of the Chestwick line? Picking up the hem of her skirts, she marched toward Lord Chestwick's private study. She slowed her pace as she approached the doorway. Smiling at the footman who stood guard at the entrance, Diana said, "A good afternoon to you, Paul."

The footman bowed. "My lady."

"Would you mind fetching Annie? It's time for us to head back home." Annie wasn't her lady's maid, but it was known between households that Paul had a hankering for Annie, who was one of the Malbury housemaids. Diana wasn't a matchmaker, but she was always happy to involve herself in such schemes if it brought harmony between the two estates.

"Stop loitering in the doorway. Come in. Come in." The earl's quill was flying across the parchment before him. Not bothering to look up, the man that was more like a papa to Diana than her own said, "I've devised a new treasure hunt for you."

Diana raced over to the desk and flopped into the seat facing the earl. "Am I to decipher a section of prose, or shall it be a poem this time?"

Exploring the extensive library in search of clues to solve the earl's puzzles was her favorite pastime during the summer months. The man was extremely clever. Most of his schemes required Diana to visit multiple times in order to solve one of his ingenious word searches. Brows creased, Diana counted the number of days remaining before she, along with her sisters and mama, were to return to London. Three blooming days is all she would have to solve the dear man's latest puzzle.

"Neither." He folded the parchment in half and half again before reaching for wax and his seal. "If you remain unmarried after your first Season and return to your family estate unbetrothed, you may come back and attempt to find my most treasured verses." He waved the sealed paper back and forth in between them.

"And if I miraculously find a suitable gentleman to marry?"

"Burn it." He placed the parchment on his desk and pushed it forward to sit right in front of her. "You will be far too busy taking up residence in your husband's abode."

She leaned forward and picked up the parchment. "Why give it to me now?" Diana studied the design stamped into the red wax. The capitalized C was backward. She rotated the note.

"Our family crest created by my forefathers utilizes the ancient italic alphabet." The earl answered her unspoken question before addressing the one she had vocalized. "Perhaps as a litmus test."

Diana lifted her gaze to stare into the old man's astute but cloudy irises. "Is it your hypothesis that I shall only forgo this..." she waved the note in the air, "my love of inquiry for the love of a man."

"Indeed, it is." He stood, slowly rounded the desk, and winged his arm out for her. The earl's fragile form leaned lightly into her as he escorted her out to the foyer, where Annie was patiently waiting by the front door.

Diana's heart clenched as she turned to say her farewell. "I shall see you next summer. Be prepared to relinquish your most favored poem." She broke every societal rule and gave the old man a hug. Her intuition told her this would be the last time she would see him.

Returning her embrace, the earl rasped, "I hope you do, my dear Miss Diana. I wish it so." The tinge of melancholy in the earl's voice had Diana fighting back tears.

The heavy material of her cloak fell upon her shoulders, and she stepped back. Blinking away the moisture in her eyes, she fumbled with the buttons and then straightened her shoulders. Plastering a smile upon her face, she confessed, "I shall miss you, my lord."

The old man chuckled. "Bah. It is not I who you will miss. It will be the challenge of sneaking away undetected to solve riddles that you shall yearn for." He glanced out the open door at the gray clouds that blocked out the sun. "I shall be happy to provide you transportation back to your family estate."

"And as you well know, Annie and I prefer to walk." Diana sent up a quick prayer that the rain would hold off and that they would make it back to Malbury Manor, dry and unnoticed.

"As you wish." The Earl of Chestwick bowed, and Diana took her leave.

She and Annie trudged along the worn path in the field that would lead them back into the mayhem of Malbury Manor. Boots covered in mud and a mile closer to her destination, Diana considered the ramifications of defying her mama's edict to marry. None were as troublesome to Diana as the thought of never seeing old Earl Chestwick again.

She patted the note in her pocket that was light as a feather but, with each step she took away from Chestwick Hall, began to weigh down her coat like a boulder. She pushed her feet forward. Would the earl's heir, a highly decorated captain in the army, Randal Wilson, honor his scholarly papa's invitation for her return to Chestwick library?

Chapter One

Jaw clenched, Diana braced a hand against the cool coach window and scanned the horizon. The chill in the traveling coach had naught to do with dusk setting upon them. No—her pebbled skin was due to her mama's frosty glares, which she was attempting to avoid. With Malbury Manor nowhere in sight, Diana straightened her shoulders and settled back against the recently refurbished tufted coach seat.

Her mama, the esteemed Countess Wallace, pinned her eldest sister, Minerva, with a steely stare. "Another Season and not a single offer of marriage. Not one. Not for you. Not for your sisters." Her mama wasn't entirely heartless, merely direct according to her sister, despite evidence to the contrary. Minerva was more of a mama to all the Malbury siblings than the woman that birthed the brood of five children.

While both Minerva and her other sister Isadora flinched at their mama's statement, Diana remained frozen. Why her mama harped on about marriage was beyond Diana's comprehension. Her parents' union was riddled with hypocrisies. There was no logical reason for her or her sisters to be in a rush to bind themselves to some gentleman who would simply ignore them. Marrying was a far worse fate than being banished for the summer to their family country seat in Manchester. She stiffened as Minerva's shoulders sagged in defeat. To date, her sister had endured three dreadful Seasons. Minerva should be awarded a medal for having avoided a match based merely on her beauty or her sizable dowry.

Diana crossed her arms beneath her cloak and stuck out her chin. "It's not Minerva's fault the gentlemen of the *ton* are all simpletons."

"Is that a fact? Then pray tell, what is your excuse for failing to garner an offer from Lord Drake?" Her mama's gaze landed upon Diana.

Success! Minerva was the queen of diverting their mama's wrath away from others, but finally, Diana was able to return the favor for her sister. What a boon, especially after all of Diana and her sister Isadora's futile attempts to assist Minerva in finding a gentleman worthy of her hand. Confidence bolstered, Diana answered. "Since I'm the youngest daughter—it stands to reason that I should be the last to lure some poor man into wedlock."

"Nonsense." Her mama withdrew a gloved hand from her fur muff and patted Diana on the knee. "It is my wish to see you all happily wed and in no particular order. I believe Lord Drake would make for a wonderful husband."

Instead of rolling her eyes heavenward, Diana lowered her gaze to the spot her mama had made physical contact with her. A peculiar numb sensation seeped into Diana's bones.

"Lord Drake is blind," Isadora stated but failed to redirect the Countess of Wallace's attention away from Diana.

"Nonsense. The boy has perfect vision."

Neighbor and best friend to Diana's oldest brother, Anthony MacMillian, Lord Drake, was charming, intelligent, and easy on the eyes, but he was not the man for Diana. "I wish to wed a man who might share my affinity for literature and riddles."

The countess's eyes narrowed. "Then I shall count myself fortunate you did not declare to all and sundry that you shall marry the first man to solve a riddle that you and your sisters may have concocted."

Minerva shrunk further into her cloak. Isadora shifted forward, attempting to draw their mama's attention. "Mama, what a brilliant idea. How fortunate for us to have inherited your intellect and wit." Isadora's voice was infused with sarcasm that had their mama's gaze shifting in her direction. Before Minerva could intervene, Isadora continued, "Diana, you must heed Mama's advice and issue the challenge upon our return to London. We have all summer to craft a riddle. Oh, won't that be fun!"

The countess's lips thinned into a straight line. "Insolent chits." With a huff, she secured her hands back into her muff and closed her eyes.

Thankful the conversation was over, Diana peered once again out the window. A familiar stone structure came into sight. Diana's pulse quickened. Chestwick Hall.

Over the years, Diana had gone missing for hours, stowed away in the Chestwick library. It was her favorite pastime. She was no ninny and recognized how rare an opportunity it was for a lady to have such access to an exquisite collection of literary works. The library shelves were filled with books amassed by the Chestwick line over several generations. Her favorites dated back to the days of the Crusades.

As a descendant of scholars, Diana found it rather peculiar that the current earl had joined the army. However, if rumors were to be believed, Randal Wilson was the devil himself upon the battlefield. He was legendary—reported to have led several ingenious attacks, slaying the enemy, and saving the lives of those who followed him into battle.

Diana craned her neck as the manor became a distant speck. After a long Season of tedious social events, she longed to curl up in the large wingback chair before the hearth at Chestwick Hall and bury her nose in one of its tomes.

A sharp elbow dug into her ribs. Diana twisted to face Minerva. "What?"

Her sister leaned in closer. "Please tell me you are not considering venturing to Chestwick Hall, uninvited."

Diana pressed her lips tight together. Minerva possessed the uncanny ability to know exactly what others were thinking before they even thought it. Her sister was always two moves ahead of everyone else, and it was dastardly annoying.

Minerva attempted to adopt their mama's stern stare but failed. "Trespassing is illegal. With the old earl gone, you are no longer welcome."

Blazes—was her sister correct? Would the new Earl of Chestwick put an end to her visits? The library shelves of her family's estate were abysmal. None of the gentlemen in her linage had even bothered to invest in the crumbling country estate, let alone finance the purchase of literary volumes. "But while the Earl of Chestwick remains at war..."

Minerva shook her head. "It is rumored that the earl was wounded and has retreated to his country estate to recover." Her sister quickly glanced at their sleeping mama. "And, it is purported that Chestwick has posted warning signs of his intentions to prosecute those that dare to step foot upon his land."

Diana was fully aware of the mutterings shared amongst the ton. Her keen hearing ensured she was apprised of the latest on-dit, including the earl's newest moniker—the Beast of Chestwick. "Surely the earl wouldn't call the magistrate if he found me in the library."

"Sister, mine. The Earl of Chestwick is not some harmless scholar. He is not like his father. He is a man who has seen and caused the death of many men."

"Yes, yes, yes. The man's war strategies were professed by the War Office to be pure brilliance." Eyes wide, Diana said, "Mayhap...he never ventures to the library. Mayhap...his injuries have him confined to his rooms. I shall simply employ stealth and take extra precautions to go unnoticed."

"Unnoticed!" Minerva twisted to face her directly. "Diana Malbury. Promise me you will not visit Chestwick Hall uninvited."

Impossible. She couldn't make such a promise.

Hmm. She must carefully phrase her promise to her sister. "Minerva. I promise not to set foot upon the grounds of Chestwick Hall."

Minerva's eyes narrowed. After a few moments, her sister nodded.

Excellent. It was a rare occurrence for Diana to outwit her sister. She would keep her word—riding her mare to Chestwick Hall meant her horse's hooves would touch the grounds, not her feet. Diana tucked her chin to her chest, allowing the hood of her cloak to slide lower. There was no way her clever sisters would spy the smirk she could not contain. Eyes closed. She evened out her breathing to feign sleep. No man nor beast would prevent her from seeking out a little piece of heaven this summer. She merely needed to devise a plan to ensure her visits to Chestwick Hall were kept secret both from her family and from the beast that guarded her oasis.

CHAPTER TWO

EYES SQUEEZED TIGHT, Randall waited for the ringing in his ears to cease and for the male battle cries to recommence.

Silence.

Beads of sweat rolled down his temple and seeped into the cut that slashed across his cheek. The burning sensation was an unwelcome reminder he still lived. He should have died along with his men. Instead, he'd been knocked unconscious, left for dead, and shipped home with a note from the War Office stating his services were no longer needed. Inheriting the title and running the estate was *not* the future Randal had envisioned for himself.

Inhaling deeply, the musty, familiar scent of Chestwick Hall settled his nerves. He raised his hand to his face—his movements stalled as his fingers grazed over the rough gauze material that was wound tight about his head and covered one eye. Urgh. His hand dropped back to the counter plane. Damn, his wounds should be fully healed.

Peering through one eye, he caught a black blur scurrying about the room. "Who's there?"

"It's jus' me yer lordship." Tinged with strain, Cartwright—his bat man turned valet's gravelly voice filtered through the buzzing in his aching head.

Exerting every ounce of energy he possessed, Randal pushed himself up to a seated position. The cool wooden headboard pressed into his back. "How are you getting on?"

"I'm finkin' navigatin' Chestwick Hall is a mite more dangerous than fightin' alongside ye on the Continent, me lord." Water splashed in a basin.

Randal cringed at the rhythmic grate of a blade being run along the strop. "You best put that razor away." A shiver ran down his spine. Cartwright wasn't right in the head if he believed he'd be running a sharp object over his still inflamed cheek.

"But ye look like a bear, me lord. Wot will Mrs. Humbleworth fink."

Randal was never the housekeeper, Mrs. Humbleworth's, favorite. She believed him cold and heartless. He had overheard her calling him such the summer before he left to fight on the Continent. Most of the staff had preferred Russel, his younger brother's easy, friendly demeanor. Randal didn't believe himself to be heartless; in fact, he loved rather deeply, merely not outwardly. He wasn't cold; he simply preferred not to show his rioting emotions and refused to blubber and wax on about matters like his papa.

Randal rubbed his chin. He had grown rather fond of his beard. "How long exactly have I been incapacitated this time?"

"Jus' a day and a half, me lord, and ye won't believe the grumblings goin' on this morn." Cartwright brought over a small bowl with lathered soap, brush, and razor. "It's time ye had a good shave."

Home for over two months, he had regained the majority of his strength but still suffered bouts of prolonged sleep, which inevitably unsettled his batman. From years of on the battlefield with the man, Randal had learned to simply remain silent and let Cartwright ramble on.

Sunlight reflected off the sharp edge of the razor that Cartwright was waving about in the air as he continued, "The entire house staff are up in arms—bemoaning your orders to the game warden to shoot trespassers on sight. Mrs. Humbleworth was a bundle of nerves. She's terrified sumthin' will happen to some chit…wot was the lass's name?" Cartwright absently stirred the soap in the bowl. "Melburn. No. Masterberry. No…"

"The Malbury girls?"

"That's the ticket, me lord. Lady Diana Malbury."

"Malbury Manor sits on the far side of the estate. It's a fair distance from here." Randal swung his stiff legs over the edge of the bed and gripped the mattress as the room began to spin. He shook his head and asked, "Diana?"

"Aye. She be the youngest daughter of the Earl of Wallace. Mrs. Humbleworth said yer da enjoyed her visits immensely during the past two summers. The staff seem rather fond of the chit. Shame if she got killed."

How old could the chit be? Randal wracked his foggy mind to recall the details of the Malbury clan. The earl's eldest and heir was a couple of years Randal's junior. Why was the man's name alluding him? Randal bowed his head, praying his skill for absolute recall would return. He'd taken a beating during his last charge against the Frogs, but that had been months ago.

"What was the purpose of Diana's visits?"

"I'd not glean the reasonin', but Mrs. Humbleworth said sumthin' about the gel bringing flowers to brighten up the place and the staff missin' her singing."

"Singing?"

"Like yer ma, they say."

His mother had left this earth near on a decade and a half ago, yet Randal cringed at the mention of her. He missed her daily. She had been the only person to see him beyond his aloof exterior. If this Diana chit was anything like his mama, he'd best steer clear. After all these years, his heart had yet to fully mend from the loss of his mother.

Brushing Cartwright's hand away from his face, Randal attempted to stand, but the shooting pain in his head had him falling back against the bed. His body may have recovered; however, his head was still ailing him. Ignoring the sparks of light behind his eyelids, he heaved a deep breath and rose. "Make sure all the signs are posted and spread the word, my edict stands. No trespassing."

"Wot ever ye want, me lord." Cartwright huffed and left the bowl of shaving soap on top of the bed.

Letting his head fall back, Randal stared at the ceiling and counted to ten. "Cartwright, come back and finish what you came to do."

"I fink not me lord. I fear me thoughts of slicing your stubborn throat might be too tempting." Cartwright left Randal's chambers with a decided click of the door.

Trust his bat man to simultaneously threaten and defy him. Randal scooped up the porcelain dish, brush, and razor off the bed and padded very slowly over to the corner to place the items next to the wash basin. He unraveled the bandage from his head. Shock registered as he caught sight of his image in the looking glass. His unkempt appearance was indeed similar to that of a bear. He leaned forward and peered at his image in the looking glass—*Why had his papa entertained a young lady two summers in a row?* The man had been devoutly in love with Randal's mama.

Never in the years since her death did his papa even glance twice at another woman. Randal was acutely aware that, as the sole survivor of his family, it was time for him to marry and produce an heir. His mind was set on a marriage of convenience. He had an entire summer to conduct his research, and come next Season, he would marry.

Splashing cool water over his face, Randal ignored the pang in his heart as it rebelled against his sound plan. Fresh air and exercise would banish the ache in his chest and aid his sore head. He needed to take back control over his rampaging emotions and the voices of his family that haunted his thoughts. His parents and Russell may have been stout supporters of love, but Randal knew love was the downfall of all good men, and he wanted nothing to do with the emotion.

He dragged himself across the room and grabbed the lawn shirt that lay neatly folded upon the end of the bed. Stuffing his arms through the sleeves, he tugged the shirt over his head. He let out a deep groan as the soft material grazed against his injured face. With his features disfigured, it was a wise plan to have the marriage agreements drawn up and signed before meeting the lady. No woman of sound mind would want to marry him. Tucking his shirt into his breeches, he searched for his waist coat and jacket. Neither were in sight. Damn his valet.

Glancing at the warm sunlight streaming through the windows, Randal ignored propriety and left his chambers. With only he and the staff present on the estate, there was no need to don the extra garments that he believed superfluous. A stroll about the property would clear his mind and ease the terrible ache in his chest and head, though it would be challenging physically. If he simply repeated the statement, mayhap it would become truth.

Chapter Three

Leaning low over her mare's neck, Diana drew her dark brown cloak over her bare shoulder. Her blood pumped in rhythm with the beat of her horse's hooves. It had taken her a week to contrive a plan that would ensure she escaped Malbury Manor without detection. Seven long miserable days. With the wind grazing her cheeks, the rush of energy flowing through her was exhilarating.

Eyes narrowed, Diana spotted sunlight glinting off a metallic object in front of her. She adjusted her seat and slowed her mount to a trot. Cautiously approaching, she found a prone form laying in the meadow. Sliding down from her mare, Diana raced to the side of the hulking man lying on his back.

"Sir." Diana dropped to her knees, barely brushing his hip. She leaned over and placed her forefinger under his nose. "You're alive." She methodically ran her hands over his shoulders and down each arm. No sign of blood or protruding bones. She pressed her hands against his chest, then lowered them to graze over his flat stomach.

Nothing was amiss, and her heartbeat began to steady. Shifting her weight, she leaned over to check each leg. Nothing broken. Turning around, she sat back on her heels and stared at the handsome, bearded stranger. The facial hair intensified her interest. Deducing the reason for his unresponsive condition must be a head injury, the trickiest of wounds to treat, Diana released a sigh and shuffled forward until her knees were parallel with the man's shoulders. "Sir. I'm going to examine your head."

Having read in medical journals the importance of immobilizing a fallen man's neck, she rose on her knees and gently placed her thumbs on his temples, and threaded her fingers through his short-shorn hair to feel his scalp. Relieved not to have come in contact with either warm oozing or dried blood, she pulled back and brushed the man's hair away from his forehead. She gasped at the sight of a large gash upon his brow.

Diana searched the nearby surroundings. There were no obvious tracks other than those freshly made by herself and her mare. What was she to do? If there were a bandit about, it would be a huge risk to leave the man alone to go for help. Her gaze flickered over the man's features. He appeared at peace. His features seemed familiar, yet she was certain she'd never met the man. Would he have kind eyes if they were to open? A person's eyes were windows into their souls. *Blast.* Minerva or Isadora would have already calculated the odds of his survival and devised some clever plan to assist the man. Instead, she was waxing poetic thoughts over the man's eyes.

"What am I to do with you?" Diana cupped his cheek, and the stranger's eyelids twitched. "Sir?"

The cool breeze fluttered the man's dark mahogany tresses, drawing her gaze back to his horrible injury. She was no physician, but she was knowledgeable enough to know that slumbering was not ideal for head injuries. She needed to wake him.

Involuntarily, she ran her thumb across his lower lip. Soft but firm. What would it be like to be kissed by those lips? Kissed! The man was dying, and she'd let her mind wander once more. Curiosity was her weakness. A quick scan of her surroundings confirmed they were still alone, and before reason set in, Diana bent over the fallen man and pressed her lips to his. When his lips parted, she snapped back to stare at him grinning at her.

"I'm surprised by your choice of methods to rouse a man, but I'll not complain. I confess it was a challenge to remain still during your examination."

"You beast!" Diana planted her hand on his chest to push herself to her feet.

With cat-like reflexes, he managed to sit upright and haul her into his lap, all in a matter of moments. Stunned, Diana remained mute as she stared into the peculiar eyes that had preoccupied her thoughts for the past year. What she had thought of as artistic flair was indeed reality—the man did have gold in his eyes.

The stranger, who she was fairly certain was the Earl of Cheswick, wrapped his arms about her tight. "I've been called worse. The quandary is how shall I refer to you? Sprite? Sorceress? Princess?"

Ha. The man had obviously not heard the moniker the *ton* had already given Diana—the Belle of Bluestockings. It wasn't as terrible as Ice Queen, given to Minerva, or Willful Wallflower, born by Isadora. "I'm not a mythical creature or a witch, and I'm most certainly not of royalty. You may call me Diana."

He rose with her in his arms and then deposited her on her feet. "Lady Diana Malbury?"

She took a step back and clasped her hands behind her back. "Aye. That is my name."

He scanned the field. "What the devil are you doing on my land?"

"I was on my way to search your library for clues. You see, your papa gave me a puzzle to solve." She patted her coat pocket that held the sealed parchment she'd held onto all Season. "He said I may return to complete it only if I remained unwed." She glanced up to find the earl's dark eyebrows slashed downward. The back of her neck prickled. Her natural instinct was to take another step back, and so she took a half step forward and poked her finger in his hard chest. "You should be thanking me for finding you."

His gaze flicked to the path that led into the forest to their right. It was where she had emerged from. "Did you see anyone as you approached?"

"Nay, it was the reflection of your buttons that caught my attention." She glanced down at the shiny silver objects. When she raised her eyes back up, his attention was back on her. A fluttering she read about a hundred times occurred in her chest. "I checked for signs of your attacker, but there were no footprints nor hoof impressions. Do you remember what happened?"

"I was patrolling the perimeter. I spun at the sound of someone sneaking up behind me, and then all I saw were stars and then blackness. That is until the moment your hands were upon my body."

Heat rushed to her cheeks. She turned to scan the ground, hiding her reaction to his statement. "Mayhap, you turned too fast and became dizzy, lost your balance, and fell." She pointed her toe and swung her foot in an arc in front of her. "It's quite plausible. You could have simply fallen and gashed your head upon a stone." But there were no objects in sight that she reasonably could deduce that would cause the nasty gash on his forehead.

"My injuries have caused dizzy spells in the past; however, I'm not convinced that is what transpired here today."

She turned and asked, "Why would anyone want to attack you? You are home on British soil, not on some battlefield upon the Continent."

"A very valid point, Lady Diana." He smiled at her, causing the fluttering sensation to return.

Odd that she had endured an entire Season surrounded by gentlemen, and never once did she experience the light fluttering sensation and, here she stood with a veritable stranger, and she'd experienced it twice. Grabbing the earl by his hand, she tugged him over to her mare. "We should return to Chestwick and clean up your wound."

Without hesitation, he lifted her up into the saddle and proceeded to mount behind her. He raised the reigns and asked, "May I?"

"Do you always ask after you have already presumed the answer?"

"I normally don't ask." He wrapped an arm about her waist and nudged her mare forward.

THANK GOODNESS HE was a skilled horseman. He needed to get the lady to safety, but having the woman seated in front of him, between his legs, her lush form pressed up against his chest, had blood rushing to his loins and his head pounding. Someone had dared to attack him on his own land.

Diana looked over her shoulder. "I am quite an accomplished equestrian."

"Beg pardon?" Damn the lack of blood flowing to his brain.

"Must you hold on to me so tightly?"

No. She was obviously skilled in the seat.

But the answer was yes. He liked having her in his arms.

However, he wasn't about to share either answer with her. Gathering her closer, he said, "I wasn't aware ladies were taught to ride astride."

"Are you intentionally trying to raise my ire?"

Rounding the bend and heading straight to the stables, Randal nuzzled closer to her ear. "You don't appear to be a lady easily influenced." He let his lips graze the outer rim of her ear. The action was to unsettle Diana, but he found it was he who was shifting his seat. "From your precise inspection of me earlier, I'd wager you were more of the logical sort with a propensity to take risks."

She stiffened in his arms. A large lump formed in his throat, and the urge to retract his statement was overwhelming. He'd never regretted words uttered prior. He prided himself on only speaking the truth, no matter how harsh.

A stable boy came running to assist them. "Lady Diana!"

"Paddy, it is so good to see you." Diana gave the boy a warm smile and added, "My, you have grown since I saw you last."

Randal handed the boy the reins. Did she know the names of all his staff? It had taken him weeks to learn all the new staff's names, and with his muddled brain, he still occasionally made a hash of referring to them correctly. Why he had a need to form a bond with his servants was baffling; however, it had become important to his sanity.

He briefly released her to slide down to the ground. Randal reached up to assist her. His breath caught at the sight of her beaming smile. Diana leaned over and placed her hands upon his shoulders. She had a tiny waist that molded to his palms. He took his time lowering her to her feet. He wasn't one to waste time, yet this woman made him want to linger in the moment.

Her hand slid up along his shoulder and neck to cup his cheek. "Will you allow me to tend to your wound?"

He flinched as her palm touched his hidden wound beneath his beard.

Diana snapped her hand away and peered intently at his cheek. "What pains you?"

"An old wound. Naught for you to worry about." He pressed a kiss to her worried brow. The small gasp behind him was the reminder he needed—they were not alone. "Paddy, give Lady Diana's mare a good brush down."

"Aye, me lord." The boy hurried off, leading the horse further into the stables.

He waited for Diana's rebuff or, at the very least, lecture on gentlemanly behavior. Instead, she tilted her head and asked, "Is it the wound that required you to return home?" Not waiting for a reply, Diana looped her arm through his and led him toward the terrace doors.

The old familiar feeling of being the outsider in his own home promptly returned. He extracted his arm and stepped away from the woman that had his mind and body in disarray. "I'll grant you access today and today only. However, you are to limit your visit to the library, and I shall have one of the footmen escort you home when you are ready." He spun on his heels in the opposite direction. He had taken two steps before he was poked in the back. Did the woman have no sense? Everyone was aware of how risky it was to provoke an injured animal, least of all a beast like him.

"How very generous of you to believe I could solve one of your papa's puzzles in a matter of hours." She released a deep sigh, "You have overestimated my abilities."

He swung around to face the impertinent chit and was hit with a pang of guilt at the sight of Diana's sad, desolate features. Diana wasn't mocking him; no she was speaking plainly and was obviously performing complex evaluations within her mind.

Diana placed her hands on her hips and muttered, "To date, I've only succeeded to solve one of his puzzles within a week. All the others took at least a fortnight, and that was with me visiting every day and him assisting me. If I involve Minerva or Isadora, perhaps..."

He held up a hand to stall her monologue. "Lady Diana. I posted those no trespassing signs for a reason. I do not wish for visitors at this time."

"But Lord Chestwick, your papa..."

He ran a hand through his hair. His actions delayed the rest of her retort, but the woman was not easily deterred. Diana took a step closer and continued, "Oh. You really believe there could be danger lurking about. Here, in the Manchester countryside."

He wasn't certain. There was no clear reason for someone to attack with the stealth required to sneak up on him, yet he couldn't quite believe he simply took a tumble. "My need for privacy has nothing to do with today's events. Perhaps it's best I simply have Paul escort you home now."

She pulled out the parchment from her pocket. "Nay. I need to discover the answer to your papa's puzzle. It's important to me. You can't deny me access to the library, especially after I endured an entire Season, remained unwed per his requirements, all for this opportunity."

"You declined offers of marriage in order to partake in some silly puzzle my papa formulated?"

Her brow creased into a frown for a brief moment. She flickered her gaze heavenward. "Your papa was a brilliant man. Kind. Loving. And he...well, I believe he understood my passion for seeking out knowledge. Not the awareness gained from studying the words on the page but the underlying truth beyond the literal meaning of script upon a piece of parchment."

Good lord, the lady communicated in poetic verses just as his papa had. "One day of full access to the family library. No more."

"Very well, step aside." She marched through the terrace doors without a backward glance.

His feet wanted to follow Lady Diana, but he remained rooted to the spot. His papa had been well aware he'd not live to see another summer—what had the old man bequeathed to the young lady?

Chapter Four

HANGING PRECARIOUSLY FROM the ladder, Diana stretched to reach the ancient volume. *Achoo.* Dust tickled her nose once more, but she held back the second sneeze.

Diana spied Mrs. Humbleworth below. The housekeeper wrung the corners of her apron. "Me lady, ye best be careful, or ye might fall."

Paul, whose shoulders now filled out his footman's uniform, had his arms stretched out in the event he might have to catch her. She gave him a confident smile and returned her attention to the book that barely brushed the tips of her fingertips. With the tips of her toes on the edge of the rung, Diana slid her hand up the spine of the book she believed might hold the next clue. She pulled the heavy tome toward her, but she found herself struggling to find her footing.

"Bloody hell! What are you doing up there?" Lord Chestwick's thunderous voice boomed from below.

Rather than holding on tighter to the ladder, Diana pulled the precious volume to her chest and let go. Eyes closed, she let herself float down into the beast's arms. She didn't trust many, but she had an innate desire to trust this man—and to test him.

"Oomph" Muscled arms caught her. She opened her eyes and immediately sought out the green and gold flecks she'd seen earlier.

"You could have broken your neck if I hadn't arrived."

"Nonsense. Paul would have caught me." She glanced at the footman and then back to the brawny beast that held her. Lord Chestwick was not at all like the indolent gentlemen she had been introduced to this past Season. He was a warrior. Bah. She needed to rein in her fanciful thoughts. The dark scowl upon Lord Chestwick's rugged features reminded her he was no knight in shining armor. No, the man was a mercenary, an extremely displeased one at that. "My thanks, Lord Chestwick, for intervening. You may release me now."

She wiggled, and the man tightened his hold of her. "Why would you trust a complete stranger?"

"Mayhap, it wasn't trust." His arms tensed beneath her knees. She shouldn't take delight in aggravating the man. Frowning to cover the smirk that threatened to appear, Diana said, "What if you foiled my clever plan?"

"Pray tell, what scheme did I thwart by saving your neck?"

She glanced up at the ladder. The ceilings at Chestwick Hall were of massive size, no doubt due to the fact the males in the family tended to be well above average height. She estimated she hadn't been more than nine feet above the ground. "It's more likely I'd have sprained an ankle than sever my neck from that elevation."

Lord Chestwick stared at her neck. "You would risk injury for what purpose?"

She lifted the book from her chest. "For the opportunity to solve your papa's mystery."

He carried her across the room, toward the door. Fearing he meant to send her away, she wrapped her left arm about his neck and tugged on his left earlobe. "You granted me the day to attempt to solve your papa's puzzle."

That stalled the man. He stopped at the threshold and deposited her on her feet. "The day grows late. Your time is up."

"But it's summer. There are at least three more hours of sunshine. I've only managed to decipher but one of your papa's clues." She wasn't about to be tossed out of Chestwick Hall until she'd given it all her effort to solve the blasted riddle.

"How many clues are there?"

She loosened her hold on the volume still pressed to her chest and pulled out the folded parchment from her décolleté. Diana cleared her throat and, from memory, recited the missive old Lord Chestwick had penned for her.

"Dear Lady Diana, Congratulations on surviving your first Season. I trust that if you are reading this, you have kept a level head and refused, I'm certain, no fewer than two proposals. But I promise the treasure you shall find will be worth the sacrifice." She peered up to find Lord Chestwick's features as hard as stone. Continuing on, "In order to discover the location of your prize, you must first decipher the following eight clues."

"Eight!" Lord Chestwick held out his hand. "Give me that damn note."

Reluctantly, she handed over the missive.

"Why would my papa devise such an intricate scheme?" Her host's eyes continued to scan the sprawling script. "What is this treasure you are to find?"

"Your papa was aware of my fondness for codes and search and finds. The more challenging, the more satisfaction I gain from solving it. Given the terms, he'd not insult me with an easily solved puzzle." She took back the note and placed it securely in the valley between her breasts and her gown. "As for the treasure, I can only hope it is his most valued piece of literature he bemoaned on and on about."

Lord Chestwick rubbed his temples. "Lady Diana, would it pain you to not speak in riddles and rhymes."

How could the man standing before her be the product of the kind, patient, scholarly man who delighted in verbally sparring with Diana and shared her passion for the unlimited possibilities of the written word?

She shoved the heavy volume into Lord Chestwick's chest. "My apologies. It appears all the years you chose to spend away upon the Continent have dulled the quick mind your papa claimed you possessed. Let me explain, over the past two summers, the two that saw your papa's health decline rapidly, the two that you did not make an appearance, I was here. And your papa claimed there was a singular poem that he was certain would explain my conundrum regarding love and marriage."

"And my papa believed…" Lord Chestwick peered down at the book in his possession, "you would find the solution in *The History of Linguistics*?"

"No, silly." Diana shook her head. "That is merely one part of the puzzle I'm to solve. I believe the poem I'm to discover is stashed between the pages of the last clue."

"Why did he not simply tell you who penned this elusive piece of literature?"

"Ahh…where would the fun be in that?" She reached to reclaim the book. "Also, your papa claims it was written by a scholar who remains in hiding and has declared they shall remain until the poem's true meaning is discovered."

Lord Chestwick's eyes widened. "You can't believe in all this nonsense."

Diana tugged at the book. Instead of relinquishing it, Lord Chestwick deftly placed it behind his back. The momentum pushed Diana a step closer, and he wrapped an arm around her waist to bring them face-to-face.

Diana stared into his hazel eyes. "Why would your papa lie?"

"Mayhap, he created the elaborate story as a hoax. Mayhap he was suffering from an aging disease."

"Aging disease!" Diana roared. "How dare you accuse your papa of misleading me. You know nothing. For years you have been off fighting in the war. Not once did you return to visit, even when you were alerted to your papa's heart condition."

Lord Chestwick flinched but remained inches away. "I couldn't abandon my men."

"Couldn't or wouldn't?" Her challenging statement rolled off her tongue without thought. Old Lord Chestwick had loved his son unconditionally, even made excuses for his absence. Diana couldn't comprehend why Randal had remained abroad rather than returning home.

He released his hold on her and took a step back. "I was responsible for the lives of many." With the book held tightly in both hands behind his back, Lord Chestwick began to pace the width of the doorway. "My papa wrote to me. He disclaimed the severity of the surgeon's assertions." Confusion and pain flickered in Lord Chestwick's eyes.

Diana stepped in front of him and placed a hand upon his upper arm. "Of course, he did. Your papa didn't want to add to your burden." She guided the distracted Lord Chestwick back over to the settee.

Guilt and sorrow weighed heavily in her chest. Weak-kneed, she sank down to sit and adjusted her skirts. "You truly didn't know how dire his health was. I apologize." She patted the empty spot next to her. Absently, Lord Chestwick offered her the book and squeezed into the space she had invited him to occupy.

He leaned forward, resting his elbows upon his knees. "I should have suspected..."

Uncertain of how to provide comfort to the man she had only met a few hours prior, Diana drummed her fingers over the volume that kept her leg from bobbing up and down from nerves.

Lord Chestwick raised his head to gaze out the windows. "The sun shall be setting soon—won't your family be looking for you?"

"Mayhap." Diana wasn't ready to leave. She wanted to console the man that she had falsely accused of being a heartless son. If she engaged his help to solve his papa's last puzzle, would it assist him with closure? She flipped the book open. "Minerva will know to come here first if I'm needed." Diana retrieved the missive once more from her bodice and studied it closely.

Lord Chestwick shook his bowed head. "You have no intentions of leaving, do you?"

"Not until I retrieve my prize."

He leaned back and crossed his arms over his chest. "If you have the correct volume, I suggest you turn to page sixty-nine."

She glanced at her host, who rolled his eyes heavenward and muttered something under his breath. "Are you certain? The clue states—Two numerals combined create three objects."

"Trust me."

She did trust him. But why she did was still befuddling. "Very well."

Diana fanned the pages until she found the numeral sixty-nine and laid the book out flat over her lap. Lord Chestwick reached for the book. His forearm brushed her chest, sending sparks throughout her entire body. She remained still, analyzing her body's reaction to the unintentional caress.

With one half of the volume on her lap and the other half on his, Lord Chestwick peered at the content of the page. He appeared unaffected by the intimate touch. How infuriating.

His gaze shifted to the slip of parchment in her hand. "May I?"

"Of course." Diana grazed the side of her breast against his outstretched hand as she handed him the clues.

Lord Chestwick's breath hitched, and his gaze dipped to the décolleté of her dress. A thrill ran down her spine with the knowledge she, too, could evoke a reaction from the man. He wasn't as oblivious as he portrayed himself to be.

Grinning, Diana asked, "What three objects do you suppose we are searching for?"

He blinked twice before saying. "This was a terrible idea." He glanced up to look out the windows, where the last rays of sunlight were quickly disappearing.

He growled, "I shall summon the carriage." He stood, and his gaze drifted to the tops of her breasts once again. "You are not to return uninvited. Am I clear?"

"Aye. In the future, I shall simply await your invitation..." She gave him a broad smile. "That is to resume my pursuit of the poem, of course." She returned her attention to the book before her and made no effort to leave.

Lord Chestwick's brow knitted into a deep frown. He was no doubt accustomed to soldiers obeying his every command without question. However, Diana was not one of his men, and by denying her access to the library, the man had declared a different type of war...one Diana was set on winning.

Chapter Five

Infuriating woman. Randal ran a hand through his hair and stomped out of the library. He needed to put distance between himself and the lovely Diana. A scurry of footsteps preceded him, and the front door was flung open. Stepping outdoors, Randal halted two steps past the threshold, and he bent at the waist. He inhaled deeply, seeking to calm his rioting emotions as he rested his hands on his knees.

Maintaining control had never been an issue in the past. A strength that had served him well in the war. Yet thirty minutes in the presence of Lady Diana, and he had lost all semblance of logic and propriety. He straightened to his full height. It shouldn't have been a struggle to release the woman. His lips curled at the corners. It had taken every ounce of self-discipline to rein in his instinctual reaction to kiss the brazen woman who dared to touch his ear.

The prickle along the back of his neck was a familiar feeling he'd experienced many a time over the years. Wiped of energy, he scanned the grounds. There was danger lurking close by. Randal raised his hand to touch the increasing lump on his forehead. Had he been attacked, or had the dizzy spells returned?

Randal turned to go inside and do battle once more with the woman who endangered his sanity. Lady Diana was the first person to ever challenge him the way she had. All too often, people were more than happy to relinquish control and their responsibilities over to Randal. Her rebuff injured his ego more than he cared to admit. With one hand on the library door handle, Randal closed his eyes and visualized the missive his papa had neatly penned.

An image of the tops of Lady's Diana's soft, voluptuous bosom edged out his thoughts of the ridiculous riddle his papa had devised. Each clue had references his papa had drawn upon when the old man, long ago, attempted to explain to Randal how a child was conceived and how a gentleman prevented such a happenstance. More befuddling was why Lady Diana would forgo marriage to solve such nonsense?

Randal pushed the door open ready to begin his interrogation and obtain the answers he sought. All queries fled his mind as he entered the library to find Lady Diana dangling once again from the ladder. The tips of her fingers slipped off the wooden rung. Even with his long strides, he was too far to reach her in time before she hit the floor. He'd watched men fall to their death, but the sight of Lady Diana tumbling through the air had him holding his breath as she landed awkwardly on one foot and fell back, her head hitting the padded arm of the settee.

He rushed to her side. "Lady Diana?"

Eyes fluttering open, Diana said, "I told you I wouldn't break my neck." She lifted her head and attempted to lean up on her elbows.

"Aye, you were right." The lump lodged in his chest remained as he gently slid his arm under her to assist her to a sitting position.

She clenched her skirts in her hands, raising the hem. Her foot rested in an odd angle. "It appears my ankle might not have fared as well as I'd hoped."

He placed an arm under her knees and picked her up. "I'll send for a physician."

"Oh, no need to go to the trouble." She smoothed out her skirts as he settled her upon the settee. "If you could send word to Malbury

Manor, I'm certain Minerva will make the necessary arrangements for my transportation home."

He fetched a pillow from the wingback chair and gently placed it under her injured ankle. What the bloody hell was he doing fussing over her like a besotted fool. He should simply do as she asked and allow her family to tend to her wounds. Hovering over Lady Diana, he asked, "Is your sister trained to assess your injuries?"

"Don't be silly, women are not allowed to attend university, let alone the Royal College of Physicians." Lady Diana leaned back and calmly clasped her hands in her lap. "However, my brother Gregory is completing his final year at Oxford. He's due to arrive tomorrow or the day after at the very latest. He will be able to tend to my injury."

Lady Diana's tranquil demeanor only rankled his. "In that case, you shall remain here until your brother arrives." Randal forced himself to relax but kept his hands firmly clutched behind him. The urge to pick her up, settle her upon his lap, and hold her close had his mind and body at odds with each other.

Lady Diana was nothing like the tittering young debutantes or the mind-numbing ladies he recalled having been subjected to the last time he was in London for a Season. The woman was not unsettled by silence; she spoke with a purpose and was blessed with wit and humor that he understood. A jolt to his heart had his pulse racing. He wanted Lady Diana to stay.

She narrowed her gaze at him. "Have you lost your wits? I can't stay here unchaperoned."

She had a valid argument, but he wasn't about to change his mind. He turned about, tearing his gaze from her pretty, upturned face and pretended to look about the room with interest. With one eyebrow arched, he asked, "You are currently sans a companion, are you not?"

"Aye, but that's because I had planned to sneak back into Malbury Manor during supper." Her cheeks flushed a light pink color. "Is there any possibility you would agree to send a discrete message to my sister instead of alerting my mama?"

Tempted to say yes simply to make her happy, Randal shook his head decisively. The minx was clever, but she needed to learn that there were consequences for such risky schemes. "Not a chance."

"Have you considered that my papa will demand marriage if it is discovered that I've spent more than the socially acceptable quarter-hour?"

The consequences of him allowing her to remain under his roof had flittered through his thoughts hours ago. Marriage to Lady Diana seemed rather intriguing rather than disturbing. It was expected he would be on the hunt for a bride this upcoming Season. Mayhap he could avoid another disastrous Season and wed over the summer. "We are in the Manchester countryside, not on Governors Square. There are no prying eyes on the hunt for scandal." He walked over to the writing desk in the corner and retrieved a piece of parchment from the drawer. Searching for a writing instrument, he pulled the side compartment open.

From behind, Lady Diana asked, "Are you searching for this?"

He turned in time to view Lady Diana retrieving a wooden pencil from her hair. Long brown tresses fell about her shoulders. His hand twitched. What would it be like to thread his fingers through that hair? To have those locks fall over his naked body. Randal wasn't one to indulge in fantasies. He prided himself on being well grounded; however, his imagination was proving to be hard to overcome. He cleared his throat and rubbed his temples.

"Lord Chestwick, is your head aching?"

It wasn't his head upon his shoulders that was throbbing. "Nay." He shifted to ensure she wouldn't spy the bulge in his pants. He opened a second compartment and released a breath. His papa's quill and ink remained neatly stored away. Randal's hand paused as he reached for the writing instrument. Had his papa purposefully challenged Lady Diana, knowing he would be captivated by her temperament? Bah. His papa was no interfering matron.

The rustle of material behind him spurred him into action. Refocused on the task at hand, he dipped the quill in the dark liquid. Would Lady Diana's parents insist upon a union?

He proceeded to pen a long and detailed message informing Countess Wallace of her daughter's misadventures. After reading over the missive, Randal picked up the parchment and crumpled it into a ball. A mutually agreed upon marriage of convenience was what he sought, not a forced union due to some arbitrary etiquette rule.

Randal dipped the quill once more. Poised to attempt to draft another note, he stared at the blank page and waited for the appropriate words to form in his mind. Instead of prose, images of Diana's long tresses strewn across his pillows invaded his thoughts. Mayhap marriage to Diana would be the best solution.

Chapter Six

SEATED UPON THE settee, Diana idly rolled the pencil between her thumb and forefinger. What did the beast intend to say in his missive? Her mama would leap at any plausible excuse to marry her off. Diana inhaled and, as she exhaled, she relaxed each of her fingers that were tightly gripped around the writing instrument she often used as a hair pin. If only there were some way she could ensure Minerva would intercept the note. Her sister would know exactly how to sneak Diana back into her parents' home. Absently, Diana tapped the end of the pencil against her chin. There was naught she could do about the content the man was drafting.

The material of Lord Chestwick's jacket stretched taut across his back. The man's impressive build brought images of the Elgin Marbles Diana had viewed while in London. There was no time for daydreaming. She placed the rejected writing instrument between her teeth and rubbed the back of her head over the spot that throbbed. It was a good thing she hadn't injured more than her ankle, which radiated with pain. Diana raised her hands to twist her hair back into a makeshift chignon and stabbed the pencil back through her hair. What was the man crafting, a novel? Arms crossed, she waited for her host to finish.

Diana focused on calculating the odds of Minerva intercepting the missive. If her sister failed to do so, Diana was certain Lord Chestwick would find himself leg shackled quicker than either of them could blink. She would be forced to marry the man whose eyes haunted her days and her nights. All Season, she had carried the sealed missive and the image of eyes with green and gold flecks with her. She wasn't a believer in fate or destiny. The Malburys were believers in science. Her papa and her eldest brother Benedict were botanists, which aided them in managing the estate.

Her mama and Minerva, talented strategists. Gregory was to be a physician. Isadora was a talented mathematician, and Paul, the only sibling younger than she, was an avid astronomer. Her family was a methodical lot and often approached life with precision that left Diana baffled.

Her lips thinned into a straight line. Her sisters evaded the rules of etiquette with complex schemes. However, would Minerva be able to conceive an elaborate ruse that would prevent Diana's presence alone with Lord Chestwick from becoming the latest on-dit? Etiquette would dictate Diana was already embroiled in a scandal—a lady should never find herself alone with a gentleman in a room, let alone an entire estate. The thought of being bound to the man that dwarfed the chair he was seated in sent a warm swath of contentment throughout her, rather than the ice-cold fear that had tricked down her spine upon being introduced to each eligible gentleman during her first Season out.

She swung her legs over the edge of the settee and gingerly placed her feet upon the floor. "After contemplation, I believe I'm well enough…" The searing pain that shot up her leg cut off the rest of her thoughts. She inhaled sharply and began to count down from fifty in the hope the pain would subside.

Swooped up into the air, she opened her eyes to find herself once again wedged tightly against Lord Chestwick's solid chest. "Put me down." The man moved fast. The pain hadn't even abated before she was back in his arms. When he ignored her demand, she added, "I'm too heavy and too old to be carried about like a babe."

"I've carried men three times your size off the battlefield. Please stop wiggling."

As they crossed the library door threshold, Diana asked, "Where are you taking me?"

His angered look confirmed her suspicion—the man was not used to being questioned.

"If you intend to carry out your threat and summon my mama, then I must be in the drawing room, at the very least, with a maid or a footman present in the room, or you shall be standing before a reverend by month's end."

His steps slowed. "Very well. The green drawing room it is. But you must promise not to try and leave. You will only do further harm to your ankle."

Nestled in his arms, she had forgotten about the throbbing pain. "Aye. I promise."

They passed Paul standing at attention in the hall. Lord Chestwick stopped and took three steps back. "Please send word to Mrs. Humbleworth to meet me in the drawing room. Then go to the icehouse and fetch me a bowl of ice, along with several washcloths."

"Aye, me lord." Paul raced off.

"What is the ice for?"

"I've read theorems that applying ice to a sprain will reduce swelling and pain." He resumed walking down the corridor.

When and where had he read such propositions? He had been on the Continent fighting in a war, not studying medical journals. She was jostled slightly as he turned to squeeze through the significantly smaller door that led to the drawing room.

Lord Chestwick slowed his pace and peered down at her. "If you believe it unwise to alert your family to your injury, what do you propose?"

Finally, he understood the risk he was taking with both their futures. Her mind went blank. She had no plan. All she knew was now that she had gained access to the library, she didn't want to leave. Diana hadn't planned on incurring an injury. She had simply been calculating the risk of falling when her foot slipped off the rung as she went to replace the heavy volume. The throbbing ache in her ankle was bearable, but she couldn't be certain whether or not her ankle was, in fact, broken. Diana met Lord Chestwick's searching gaze. "An impromptu house party?" If she had learned anything about Randal in her short time in his home, it was he had a strong distaste for company. She was betting on that knowledge.

His muscles tensed, bringing her nose-to-nose with the man. He looked directly into her eyes. "You must have lost all your wits when you hit your head earlier."

Ignoring his retort, Diana pleaded her case. "You could invite my sisters, and I believe our other neighbors, Lord Drake and Lord Cunningham, are already in residence at their country estates."

"Absolutely not." The stubborn set of his jaw was a challenge.

To prove her theory that Randal would be more amicable to a sensible solution, Diana said, "If you recall, I made the suggestion of contacting my sister Minerva. She is a skilled strategist. She will know exactly what to do."

He lowered her to the chaise lounge. "Mrs. Humbleworth, thank you for coming." The man had excellent hearing to have known the woman was approaching. He straightened and turned to face the housekeeper.

Diana peered around his large form and smiled.

Mrs. Humbleworth bobbed a quick curtsy, her brows furrowed as she faced her employer, then glanced back at Diana, who gave the housekeeper a wink. The tension in the woman's forehead eased.

Lord Chestwick cleared his throat, bringing Mrs. Humbleworth's attention back to him. "I need you to discreetly alert Lady Minerva that her sister has requested her aid."

"Are ye all right, Lady Diana?"

"I'm well. I simply rolled my ankle. However, Lord Chestwick is requesting I remain here for a spell. I'd appreciate your assistance in sending word to Minerva via the backdoor."

The housekeeper's gaze flickered to her employer and then back to Diana. "Of course, my lady. I'll send Willie over at once."

Mrs. Humbleworth curtsied and passed Paul on her way out. The footman brought forward the tray with the items Lord Chestwick requested.

With his back to her, Lord Chestwick barked, "Remove your slipper and stocking." He removed his jacket, flung it through the air to land on the back of a chair, and began rolling up the sleeves of his lawn shirt.

"I beg your pardon?"

"I need to apply the cold pack to your injury."

She leaned forward to do as he bid, but her attention was on her host. He dipped his fingers into the bowl and retrieved several chipped pieces of ice and wrapped them up in a washcloth. Careful not to allow the ice to escape, he placed it in one hand, palm up. Taking the two steps to the chaise, he knelt and gently laid the compress over her skin, which was turning a garish blue-purple color.

He shook his head. "You won't be walking for at least a week."

"Do you think it is broken?"

"I'm not a trained physician nor a surgeon. I've only assisted those injured on the battleground. The good news is that there is no bone protruding from your skin."

"Well, I guess that is fortunate." She didn't want to imagine the gruesome sights he must have seen while fighting the French. The question of why Lord Chestwick had chosen to enlist and place his life in danger still plagued her. Mayhap if she gathered enough courage, she'd ask him.

CARTWRIGHT WAS RIGHT. Navigating the battlefield was a far easier task than dealing with the women under his roof. In battle, the goal was simple—don't get yourself killed. It was quickly becoming apparent that his new goal would be to avoid ladies of the *ton* and especially those with a surname of Malbury. Lady Diana was a quandary. Part of his mind screamed to get rid of the chit, but the other half of his brain was rebelling against logic and wished to find out more about this rather intelligent and intriguing woman.

Capturing the trickle of melted ice that ran over her delicate skin with a clean, dry linen, Randall asked, "How many offers of marriage did you decline in order to attempt to solve my papa's ridiculous puzzle?"

"What does it matter?"

It shouldn't matter. At least not to him. What did he care if she had rejected the suit of one or ten men for a silly poem? He shrugged. "I was merely curious as to how many gentlemen failed to convince you a life with them would be more interesting than solving a riddle amongst dusty library shelves."

"You best not let Mrs. Humbleworth catch you calling anything dusty under this roof on her watch." Her lopsided grin almost evoked a rumbling in his chest.

Her quick wit and sense of humor were disarming. He had little to smile about for years, including those before he set foot upon a battlefield. "Why do I get the impression that your fear of Mrs. Humbleworth's disapproval outweighs your trepidation of me?"

"Should I be scared of you?"

It was a simple question. And the answer was, sadly, yes. He was a heartless monster, responsible for hundreds of deaths. A beast devoid of emotion, capable of wiping out entire French encampments without hesitation. Had his ruthless reputation not reached her innocent ears. Was it possible she might not know his enemies referred to him, and quaked in fear at the mention of, the Beast of

Chestwick?

He leaned in, crowding her. "Mayhap."

He jumped to his feet at the symphony of voices, stomping of feet, and banging of doors. They were under attack. He reached for his sword that normally sat at his hip. Grasping air, he strode toward the door when a woman marched through the entrance to the room flanked by two men who shared the same familial features—the Malbury's were all striking in appearance just like Diana. He froze, confronted by the three.

The young lady, who had to be Lady Minerva, turned to the younger of the two gentlemen and ordered, "Gregory, cease your glaring and see to our sister." Like a well-trained soldier, the man obeyed the directive and made his way to Diana. Lady Minerva then arched an eyebrow in the direction of her other brother. If Randal's recollection was correct, the man was heir to an earldom and currently held the honorary title of Viscount Kent, Lord Benedict Kent.

Lady Minerva's lips didn't move, but the meaning of her gaze was as clear as if she had spoken the words—*Shall I, or would you prefer to handle matters?*

After garnering the barest of nods from her brother, Lady Minerva turned and faced Randal. While she was at least a foot shorter, it was as if she was looking down her nose at him, not the other way around. "Lord Chestwick, I beg your pardon for our rude intrusion into your home. I'm fully aware of your request for privacy, of course, only a dullard would pay no mind to the litany of signs placed about your estate." Lady Minerva had raised her voice, and although Diana sat behind him, he was certain the chit had winced. Without taking a breath, Lady Minerva continued, "I can assure you we shall be on our way shortly, as soon as..."

The woman's monologue was interrupted by her brother Gregory. "Change of plans, Minerva." He sat back on his heels and shifted slightly to his right.

The woman flew to her sister's side and knelt down to examine the injury herself.

Diana swatted at her sister's hands. "Ouch! Minerva, please."

Ignoring Diana, Minerva turned to the brother and surmised, "Sprained not broken."

The young Mr. Gregory Malbury nodded. "However, based on the amount of swelling and tenderness, ligaments have been torn. It will be at least three days before I can determine the exact extent of her injuries."

"Three days!" Randal was not the only one to utter the two words; the rest of the Malbury clan, Diana, Minerva, and their eldest brother, Lord Kent, all echoed his sentiments.

Mr. Malbury tilted his head toward Lady Minerva and whispered, "Benedict can carry her to the carriage, but with the four of us, it will be cramped and rather painful for Diana."

Minerva's eyes narrowed at Diana for a second. The woman's silent message that any pain endured by Diana would serve as punishment for her sneaking out was clear as if she had spoken the words out loud.

It was rather impressive that Lady Minerva was able to effectively communicate without sound. Her expressive features clearly portrayed her meaning. It was a skill he, too, had mastered over the years. He could issue orders to his men in a single glance. He was not on a battlefield, although, at the moment, he recognized there was a war waging about him. One he was unfamiliar with the rules of. It made him extremely uneasy.

To break the awkward silence, he said, "Diana may stay here for a few days."

His offer provoked Diana's oldest brother into action, who stepped forward and said, "Either we all stay, or we all leave." Lord Kent slid a quick glance at Lady Minerva over his shoulder.

Both Randal and Lady Minerva replied, "Not possible." It was rather unsettling that Diana's sister's thoughts were akin to his own. Although what was most surprising was that no one had corrected his error in failing to include the honorific of *Lady* before Diana's name.

Randal shifted his gaze back to Diana, who had intruded both into his home and his every thought. Head bent, eyes closed, and fingers pressed to her temples, Diana's lips were moving, but he couldn't hear a syllable. She was either mumbling to herself or praying for divine intervention, he didn't know which. However, it was clear she was unhappy. His heart, hardened after years of observing his men in pain and on the brink of death, began to ache at the sight of the strain on Diana's features. He had to rectify the situation. "Lady Minerva, I'm certain if we take a moment, we can come to some sort of arrangement that will suit everyone."

Lady Minerva studied Diana for a moment before returning her attention to him. "If we were to agree upon terms, it would have to ensure both that my sister's reputation remains intact, and she will have full unrestricted access to your library."

Diana's face lit up like a child given a box of sweets. She had warned him that her eldest sister was an excellent strategist. He was no dunce and was renowned for his stratagems at war. Would those assist him now? Before he could devise a plan, he'd first need to make a full assessment of the situation and garner all the pertinent details and access his opponent's skills. And Lady Minerva was suddenly the enemy—she was definitely a threat, except it wasn't Lady Minerva who threatened his peace of mind and solitude. No, it was the woman staring intently from the settee that rattled his every nerve from head to toe. He was trained to keep all parties within sight, and even from his peripheral vision, Lady Diana was playing havoc with his normally even-rhythmed pulse.

Randal placed his hands squarely behind his back. "You made mention of Diana's reputation..."

"You mean...*Lady* Diana. That is unless in the span of one afternoon you have decided to wed my sister."

Lord Kent took a step closer and whispered, "Minerva, what the devil are you doing?"

It was obvious the family was close and well aware of each other's strengths and limitations. Ignoring her brother, Lady Minerva's gaze never wavered. The woman was issuing him a dare of some sort.

Bells of alarm rang in his ears. What was the chit up to? "Given *Lady* Diana has been deemed immobile for a period of time, I don't see the need to grant her access to the Chestwick library."

"I don't recall specifying the period of access to be granted."

Lady Minerva's smile faded as Lord Kent muttered, "Stop toying with the man. Out with your plan."

"Diana and I humbly agree to accept your hospitality until the other guests arrive."

"What other guests?" Randal pierced Minerva with a gaze that had his enemies on the battlefield confessing all their secrets.

The insolent woman didn't even blink. She retorted, "Your friends and our neighbors, of course. For the house party."

Diana had made mention of a house party earlier.

"No house party." He shifted his attention back to Minerva and continued. "All of you may stay for three days, and I shall grant Lady Diana access to the library for a week once she is fully healed."

Minerva countered, "Three weeks."

"Seven days." He faced Minerva, who was proving to be a worthy opponent.

"My lord, you offend me."

"Two weeks, and that is my final offer."

Lord Kent interjected, "Agreed. I shall take my leave now and return to Malbury Manor to see to it that our parents do not interfere." He turned Minerva by the shoulders and gave her a quick hug before pulling back and saying sternly, "I shall expect you all home three days hence."

Mr. Malbury said, "You're giving orders to the wrong sister."

Peering over Lady Minerva's shoulder, Lord Kent said, "Diana, you best hope Gregory is correct in his estimation of your recovery."

"I promise to be a good patient, brother."

The familial interactions increased Randal's ire at himself for allowing the Malburys to disturb his peace. He had loved his brother, but they had not been close like the Malbury siblings crowding his drawing room. For a split second, he wondered what it would be like to have such a close bond. The familiar feeling of once again being an outsider in his own home spurred him to spin on his heels and head out of the room without a word.

He'd managed to reach the threshold when Lord Kent slapped a hand on his shoulder and said, "My thanks for letting my family reside with you while Diana recovers. Send word if you need any assistance." The man continued on ahead of him, and Randall watched as Lord Kent strode through the foyer and climbed into the Malbury coach.

The urge to run away as he had years ago when he joined the army was upon him once more. Only this time, as the sole living member of his family, he was required to stay put. He was stuck with the monstrosity of an estate that never felt like home and guests he had no idea what to do with.

Chapter Seven

Wringing her hands in her lap, Diana waited for her siblings to lecture her on her perils of sneaking into a stranger's home.

"Pray explain *exactly* how you injured your ankle?" Minerva demanded.

Minerva must feel somewhat sympathetic, for she was inquiring after her physical health and not her mental soundness. Diana shifted her gaze between her sister and Gregory. "I fell off a ladder."

"From what height?" Gregory scowled down at her. "Based on the swelling of your ankle, it was not mere inches."

Her siblings had all mastered the art of manipulating the truth with ease, while Diana struggled to veer from the facts, not in her favor. "I…It might have been a f-few feet or so."

Minerva groaned. "You had best examine her thoroughly—she's obviously not forthcoming."

Before Gregory could begin a full examination, Diana confessed, "I did hit my head."

Her brother promptly began methodically running his fingers over her head inch by inch. Diana flinched as the tip of Gregory's fingers grazed the tender knot. "Ow. Gentle. You need to learn to treat your patients with more care."

"She has a decent sized contusion on her head." He continued with his examination and added, "I'd hope my patients won't all be as reckless as you."

"Then it was a wise decision for you not to become a surgeon…" She stared back at her brother's confused features and expounded, "Surgeons are present at every duel, are they not?"

Minerva sighed. "Dueling is illegal. And so is trespassing."

Diana peeked up at her sister and smiled. "I'm sorry. You didn't have to volunteer to stay."

Minerva shook her head and began to pace from one side of the room to the other.

When her sister neared, Diana added, "You could have sent my maid and Gregory."

Minerva's steps didn't falter at Diana's statement. Her sister merely glanced at her momentarily before she proceeded to pace about the room. Gregory lowered his athletic form into the chair next to the settee and leaned forward. He braced his forearm over his knee and in a low whisper, said, "I'm certain Benedict is packing up the staff and sending them over now."

"But that doesn't explain why Minerva felt it imperative that she stayed as well?"

Gregory's sad eyes tracked Minerva. "Mama has been harping on all day about the failure of the past Season. I believe Minerva blames herself for none of you securing a husband."

"Pfftt. That's last Sunday's news." A stab of guilt for not being at home to assist in deflecting their mama's barbed comments hit Diana in the chest. "Minerva hates sleeping anywhere but in her own bed. I can't fathom why she would wish to remain here at Chestwick Hall?"

"I have a theorem." Gregory leaned in closer. "Lord Chestwick is the first gentleman to intelligently converse and, even better, dared to challenge Minerva since her first Season. Perhaps, she's considering…"

"Stop attempting to whisper." Minerva came to stand in front of Diana once more. "I'm sorry if my silly declaration of marrying the first fool to defeat me in a game of chess ruined your first Season."

"Don't be silly. I didn't want to marry any..."

Minerva placed her finger to her lips, silencing Diana. Her sister had hearing like a bat; someone must be approaching. Gregory reached out and plucked the oddly skewed pencil from her hair, and Diana's long locks fell down her back. Diana was in no mood for her brother's games. She snatched the sharp writing instrument back and was about to reach up to twist her hair back into the makeshift chignon when Lord Chestwick reentered the room.

Her host's eyes were trained upon her, as if no one else occupied the room. Randal marched directly to stand before her, and he lowered himself, taking up a position like a frog. Eye level, he softly said, "How are you feeling?"

The throbbing pain in her ankle fled from her mind as she stared into his mesmerizing eyes. Out of the three Malburys in the room, she was the worst at pretending nothing was amiss. Isadora was the worst at playacting, which was why she was normally left at home. Diana took in a slow, calming breath, attempting to settle her racing pulse, but all she could focus on were the man's uniquely colored eyes.

They were full of sincerity. Randal truly cared for her well-being, which was unsettling. There was no question that her family loved her; however, being the fifth child out of six, she often became invisible, which worked in her favor most of the time. Unaccustomed to being singled out and fawned over, Diana was acutely aware she was in her host's sights.

Diana curled her lips into a smile. "My thanks, Lord Chestwick, for extending such a magnanimous invitation to my siblings and me. It will be an honor to remain here at Chestwick Hall."

"I surmised from your sister's posture and tone, I hadn't much of a choice, or did I?"

Diana replied, "Aye, Minerva can be quite persuasive when she wishes to be. However, there was an alternative—you could have lived up to your reputation and simply had us escorted off your property."

"True. Except I didn't." For the first time since she met him, the corners of his lips twitched, almost forming a smile but not quite.

Diana imaged he'd be quite handsome if he smiled. What would his laugh sound like? *Silly.* What reason would the man have had to smile or laugh on the battlefield? But he wasn't on the Continent any longer. If she couldn't continue solving his papa's riddle, Diana settled upon herself the challenge of making Lord Chestwick laugh. He needed some joy and levity in his life.

She found the will to remove her gaze from the man in front of her, only to realize that her siblings were off in the corner whispering. Minerva's back was to them. Her sister's perfect posture meant she was scheming. Gregory's expressive face revealed he did not care for their sister's plans.

Lord Chestwick shifted, and before she realized what he was about, he picked her up from the settee and cradled her to his chest. "Mrs. Humbleworth should be done preparing your chambers."

She should be alarmed by his presumptuous behavior, mayhap even appalled, yet in his brawny arms, she was hit by the sensation that this was exactly where she should be. Safe and secure. "Do you intend to carry me about for the duration of my stay?"

"Absolutely not. You are to remain abed for three days."

The sting of his response had Diana mentally adding for him—"*and out of my way.*" Exhausted, she rested the side of her head against his shoulder as they made their way through the enormous mansion. "What of Minerva and Gregory?"

"Not to worry. I hear them behind us." One corner of his lips curled into a semi-smirk. "While your sister's footsteps are near silent, your brother's are like those of an elephant."

Her shoulders bobbed as she released a giggle. "You associated Gregory with an elephant. I must share that with Benedict."

"Why Lord Kent and not Mr. Malbury?"

"Must you use their formal names? I'd prefer you refer to my brothers by their given names, that is when no one else is present." She hoped he'd agree and drop his defenses against strangers. He had begun to address her by her given name, let her in a little.

"Why do you not simply answer my questions? You have an irritating habit of avoiding my queries while simultaneously redirecting the conversation."

"At home, Benedict is the one referred to as an elephant. He's big, strong, and has a memory that never forgets. While Gregory is thought of more like a rabbit, smaller, yet agile and extremely lucky."

"What animal did your family assign to you?"

"Oh, well, first you must know Minerva is the owl, Isadora is a deer, my youngest brother is a fox, and to answer your question, I'm a Scottish wildcat."

"Ah, so not merely a regular wildcat, but a Scottish one." His steps slowed. "Ferocious. Unpredictable and fiercely independent. From the little time I've spent in your company, I would agree you are indeed most like a Scottish wildcat." His teasing tone had her tilting her head to view him clearly.

"Based on our acquaintance, I'm fairly certain Minerva would agree with me that you, Lord Chestwick, are most like a bear. Self-contained and strong-willed."

He stopped, and instead of approaching the door, he stepped back and whispered, "I agree we should dispense with formalities, please, address me as Randal."

Gregory appeared with his arms out, ready to take over the duty of carrying her into her bedroom. She obediently shifted into her brother's arms and looked over his shoulder as Minerva bid their host a good eve and shut the door.

"I know Lord Chestwick has not been about society for some years, but Diana, you know very well how inappropriate all of this is."

"Stop worrying. There is no one here but us and Lord Chestwick.

No one will find out."

"Please do not be so naive. Household staff are notorious for gossip."

"I trust Mrs. Humbleworth."

"You trust everyone." Her sister rushed about the room, probably making sure it was just the three of them in there. Addressing Gregory, she ordered, "Put her down on the bed and go find out why our maids are delayed."

As usual, Gregory did her bidding without rebuttal. Diana waited for the latch to fall back into place before asking, "Why are you angry with me?"

"I'm not angry."

"Yes, you are. Please tell me why."

"All season, I believed it was your wish to avoid marriage. You treated every eligible gentleman as if they had the plague. Please tell me your interest in Lord Chestwick isn't merely to gain access to his library." Minerva had her hands back on her hips and was glaring at her. "Don't innocently blink at me. It might work on Lord Chestwick, but you'll not avoid the question."

"Very well. Let me explain." Diana quickly ordered her thoughts into the most logical, succinct sequence, so her sister would listen and not interrupt. "First, I found Lord Chestwick laying in the grass as I approached Chestwick Hall. He believes he was attacked, but there were no signs of another. He did admit that he continued to incur dizzy spells as a residual effect from his injuries from the war. Head injuries are tricky and should be closely monitored." Minerva nodded and remained quiet. Diana continued, "Second, I explained my purpose for my visit, and he granted me the afternoon, but the riddle bequeathed to me is far more complex than any of the others I've solved." Perhaps if she gave Minerva a compliment, it might remove the frown marring her sister's pretty features. "Mayhap, now that you are here, you could assist me."

"Flattery only works on Mama. We both know you do not really wish for my assistance. Tell me the truth—how did you fall from the ladder? You have the grace and balance of a cat."

"I admit it wasn't an accident."

"Diana Malbury!"

Diana let out a sigh of relief at the arrival of Minerva's maid, Barnett, and her own lady's maid, Fisher. They appeared, along with two footmen carrying large traveling trunks. She had gained a reprieve, but Minerva was relentless. Her sister would badger Diana until she obtained a response that explained Diana's rash actions. She did long to remain to solve old Lord Chestwick's puzzle, but it wasn't only access to the library that prompted her to risk injury. There were no words to eloquently describe the rioting, confusing emotions Randal's hazel eyes evoked within Diana—surely none she could share with her sister.

CHAPTER EIGHT

RANDAL SAT ON the edge of a wingback chair facing the fireplace in his private study. Staring at the flames with his elbows resting on his knees and a tumbler of brandy rolling back and forth between his palms, he waited for his mind to calm. Long cold nights on the battlefield, he learned to focus on the crackle of the fire and the mesmerizing flicker of the flames, allowing him to banish even the most horrific images from his thoughts. Tonight, it wasn't the sight of men falling to their death that he wished to forget; it was the terrifying image of Diana crumpled on his library floor.

The unease that had settled deep in his chest had yet to alleviate. Why seeing the small woman who had brazened her way into his home, laying hurt, was more petrifying than any other experience he'd lived through to date was confounding.

He lifted his glass and consumed the warm amber liquid as a scratch at the door echoed through the room. "Enter."

Gregory strode into the room, leaving the door slightly ajar. "Care for some company?" Diana's brother sank into the chair next to his and stretched his legs to cross them at the ankles. The man looked all too comfortable.

Randal stood and glared down at his guest. "One would think all the trespassing signs would convey my sentiments." He walked over to the sideboard and grabbed the decanter to refill his glass. Calling over his shoulder, Randal asked, "Brandy?"

"Not this eve."

Randal shook his head and raised the extra glass that was generously filled to his mouth and gulped down the drink. He'd have a sore head in the morn, but he was desperate to numb the ache in his chest. Instead of returning to his chair, he chose to stand by the fireplace, allowing him a clear view of Gregory. "From my field experience, inflammation of a twisted ankle can be assessed adequately after twenty-four hours. Why did you declare the need for seventy-two hours?"

Gregory leaned back and crossed his arms over his chest. "I was not aware you had received medical training while abroad. I'd assumed as one of Wellington's most trusted captains, you had other more pressing issues to deal with than tend to your men's injuries."

"A leader should be well versed in his men's strengths and weaknesses before going into combat." He focused on the liquid that he swirled around and around in his glass. The muscles at the back of Randal's neck tensed as he lifted his gaze to meet Gregory's knowing eyes.

Gregory asked, "If you suspected something amiss, why agree to allow us to stay?"

An excellent question. Randal wished he knew the answer. The Malburys were a perplexing lot, especially Diana. His decision to allow them all to reside under his roof had absolutely nothing to do with his befuddling reactions to her presence. Mayhap it was purely to appease his curiosity as to what exactly his papa had bequeathed to the woman.

Pushing away from the mantel, Randal replied, "I've learned over the years it is best to keep one's enemies close."

Gregory bolted to his feet. "Enemies! We are neighbors. We have no quibbles with you."

"Mayhap you do not; however, I suspect if you were to ask your sisters, their answers may differ."

"Lord Chestwick, I believe you are correct yet again." The young man's forehead wrinkled as he sank back down into his chair. "It is true, my sisters tend to consider any perspective suitors as adversaries rather than potential beaus. However, after the calamity of last Season, my mama will no doubt devise some scheme to see them all wed before they even realize what is occurring."

Before he could stop himself, Randal asked, "Why was it a disaster?"

"Pray forgive me. While you have been fighting upon the Continent, my sisters believe they have been fighting for a future that most do not believe attainable." While Diana spoke in poetry, her brother spoke in riddles. He had best stop consuming the full-flavored brandy that remained in his glass. "Mr. Malbury..."

"Please call me Greg or Malbury, everyone does but my family."

He should let the matter go, but oddly he needed to know the answer. "Very well, Malbury, what events occurred this past Season for you to declare it a disaster?"

"Hmm..."

"I find it helpful to start from the very beginning."

"Indeed. It all began with Mansville's demand that Minerva marry him. He had been her first challenger, and he claimed no other gentleman had come close to defeating the Ice Queen."

"Was it true?"

"In fairness, it did officially take Minerva twenty-two moves to defeat Mansville at chess, while it took her a mere sixteen to eighteen moves to trounce the rest."

"Exactly how many gentlemen?"

Malbury used his fingers and counted. "Four publicly known and two unbeknownst to the *ton*."

"Given that your sister remains unwed, I gather she was *not* in favor of Mansville's suit."

Malbury's shoulders slumped forward. "Minerva never told any of us why or how she concocted the ridiculous challenge for her hand. She is also extremely stubborn, and once her mind is set, there is no changing it."

"I can't believe there is no one worthy or capable of such a task."

"Oh, but there is." Malbury leaned back in his chair and pinned Randal with an unswerving stare. "Diana and I are certain of it, but the gentleman in question claims he is not suited for marriage and won't attempt to play Minerva, even if we arranged the match to be played with the upmost discretion and away from the prying eyes of the *ton*." His guest stood and paced in a tight, small circle. It was evident the family was not the type to remain still for long periods. "Until Minerva is wed, I suspect my sisters Isadora and Diana shall not agree to marry. Whether it be out of defiance to our mother's wishes or to show their support of Minerva's endeavor, it matters naught. All three of my sisters cleverly deflected the attentions of several gentlemen this past Season. And since leaving London, our mother has yet to cease bemoaning what she has deemed was the worst Season of the decade."

"There is always next Season," Randal said.

"Aye, that is true. However, if your papa hadn't interfered, I believe Diana would have been the sensible one and married this Season."

Randal's patience was worn thin. "I can only believe Lady Diana would not have married, regardless of my father's riddles."

Diana's brother's lips curved into a mischievous smile. "I guess we'll never know for certain." Malbury slapped a hand over Randal's shoulder. "The hour grows late, my lord. I shall see you in the morn."

Randal waited for the door latch to click back into place and Malbury's footsteps to fade before blowing out the breath he held and chuckled. Malbury did not know his sister as well as he thought.

If Randal assisted Diana to solve his papa's puzzle, mayhap he'd rid himself of the Malburys for good.

Chapter Nine

RANDAL PULLED A pillow over his head in an attempt to silence the ruckus of laughter that wafted through the house and permeated through the walls of his bed chamber. Memories of his childhood when Chestwick Hall was filled with fun and frivolity came rushing to mind—and ended abruptly like it had all those years ago the day his mama died.

Groaning into his pillow, Randal muttered, "Blasted Malburys."

The tinkle of feminine laughter that was fast becoming familiar and belonged to the woman who had invaded his sleep, filtered through his feathered pillow. His lips involuntarily curved into a grin—*Diana*.

In a single afternoon, she had imprinted herself upon his mind. Yes, he needed to wed, but his promise to his mama weighed heavily on his conscience. Having returned from the Continent after the parliament session had closed, he had planned to spend the summer at home recovering. Hunting for a wife could wait. There was no urgency to reacquaint himself with his peers—men and women he had very little in common with. And it was ridiculous to believe that the first lady he met would fulfill his mama's dying wish. Yes, Diana had managed to capture both his mind and his heart, but marriage was for a lifetime.

Cartwright's heavy footfalls hit the wood floors of his bed chambers and then pulled the pillow away from Randal's head. "Ye best get ready and go belowstairs." His valet held up his right arm ladened with a dark blue ensemble, and then his left arm with a deep maroon waistcoat and starched white cravat.

Randal pointed to the muted combination on Cartwright's right. "It sounds as if my guests are getting along quite fine without me." He rolled out of bed and padded over to the porcelain wash basin next to the window.

"I've known ye for four bloomin' years, and not once have ye shied away from yer responsibilities." Cartwright shook out a clean lawn shirt for him and continued, "Yer supposed to be down there hostin' or wot not, not lettin' poor injured Lady Diana perform yer duties."

"Poor Lady Diana, is it?" Randal neatly folded and replaced the damp washcloth next to the decorative bowl, a far cry from the small metal dish he'd used during the war. He returned Cartwright's glacial glare with one of his own. "The woman's injuries are self-inflicted."

Randal took his garments from Cartwright's arm one by one and donned the layers of a gentleman, not that of a soldier. While he may not be venturing onto the battlefield today, he sensed the day before him would be anything but leisurely.

Cartwright swiveled and marched over to the wash basin. "She wouldn't have taken such drastic measures if ye'd just agreed to let her use the bloomin' library." Razor in hand, his valet turned and said, "Mrs. Humbleworth thinks Lady Diana is a blessin', and I agree."

"A blessing, is she? More like a bur in one's stocking," Randal grumbled.

Soap in one hand and razor in the other, Cartwright nodded for him to sit on the bed. "I'd best make ye presentable."

Randal ran a hand over his cheek and then along his jaw. The skin was still tender beneath his beard. "I think not."

"But, me lord, ye have guests."

"I'm sure the Malburys have no objections."

Edging Randal back, Cartwright took another step closer. "I'm not referrin' to the Malburys. I'm talkin' about the other gentry that is millin' about."

Randal stood his ground and barked, "Who exactly arrived this morn?"

"Lord Kent arrived with two gentlemen in tow, a Lord Drake and another called Lord Cunningham. Oh, and Lady Diana's other sister, Lady Isadora.

His house was full of strangers. A knot the size of his fist settled in the center of his chest. "Why did you not alert me earlier?" Randal sank down and settled on the edge of the bed.

Cartwright didn't miss a beat; he expertly lathered the soap and applied it to Randal's face. "Lady Diana said ye needed yer rest after being knocked out yesterday."

Damnation. Why hadn't he sent Diana scurrying back to Malbury Manor as soon as he laid eyes on her? His first thought as he laid sprawled in the grass, looking up at her beautiful features surrounded by a halo of sunlight had been that she was an angel sent to retrieve him. Except his lips came into contact with warm, lush lips. Their brief kiss had ignited a sensation close to his heart that was familiar yet forgotten.

Another bout of laughter, this time male, rattled the walls. He should have thrown the Malbury lot out yesterday. In his brief absence, Diana had successfully laid siege upon his manor. He'd lost before he was even able to mount a defense. "I am the lord of this manor, am I not?"

Cartwright nodded. "Of course, ye are, me lord."

Randal remained still as his valet ran the razor methodically over his face, like he had done a thousand times before. Randal waited until Cartwright removed the blade and wiped it on the clean linen draped over his arm to ask, "And I remain unwed, correct?"

"Aye." His valet chuckled and nodded his head. "Ye've yet to win Lady Diana's hand in marriage."

Randal glared up at his valet. "Win?"

Brows wrinkled into a frown, Cartwright responded, "Blimey, Lady Diana was right. Ye be needing more rest. Yer not acting like yerself. Did someone sneak up on ye and knock ye senseless, or were ye takin' one of yer long naps?"

Randal had pondered over that exact question for the brief moments Diana hadn't preoccupied his thoughts. He didn't have a definitive response for his valet, which was extremely unsettling for someone who was expected to have all the answers. Randal summoned every last ounce of patience he had in order to remain seated and silent. A few more strokes of the blade, and Cartwright would be done.

His valet ran a clean washcloth over his cheek, removing all traces of soap. "Nothing hiding that scar of yers now. I'll warn ye, me lord, yer competition is mighty steep." Cartwright tilted Randal's head to the left then to the right. "Ye clean up well enough, but Lord Drake and Lord Cunningham turn a fine coat. Especially that Lord Drake. I hear the gels' hearts flutter for a gentleman with blue eyes."

Done with Cartwright's blathering, Randal stood to take his leave. "I'm not competing for Lady Diana's hand."

"Why not? I reckon Lady Diana would make a fine Countess of Chestwick." The man who had never dared to question Randal on the battlefield was frowning at him as if Randal was addled. "Yer not considering her sister—Lady Minerva, are ye?"

He knew the answer to this question at least—it was a definite no.

Randal replied, "Lady Minerva is the eldest. Why should I not?"

Returning to the wash basin to clean Randal's shaving instruments, Cartwright huffed, "Coz' she ain't Lady Diana."

His valet was correct; the two sisters were nothing alike. Lady Minerva would be an excellent choice for a wife, but it was Diana about whom he couldn't stop thinking.

Sliding his arms into the jacket Cartwright held out for him, Randal asked, "Where is the war being waged?"

"In the library."

Of course. He should have known. With a nod, he left his chambers and headed over to the west wing. The idea Lord Drake and Lord Cunningham were under his roof attempting to woo Diana had him lengthening his stride and doubling his usual pace.

DIANA SLID ONE more longing glance at the door before returning her attention back to Lord Drake, who had staked a claim in the chair opposite her. Lowering her voice to a harsh whisper, she asked, "What the devil did you say to Minerva upon your arrival that has her glaring at you?"

"Ahh...that explains why it feels like I was jabbed with a red-hot poker between my shoulder blades." Drake rolled his shoulders back and forth as if to shake off the feeling.

Frowning at the man that was like another brother to her, Diana said, "There was a time when the two of you were practically in each other's pockets. Since Minerva's debut, I can count on one hand the number of times I've witnessed you close enough to even speak to my sister. And this past Season, whenever one of you entered a room, the other fled. Why is that?"

"That is not true."

"Which of my observations are you claiming to be a lie?"

Drake grinned. "I never flee a room."

The man was a terrible liar. He tugged at his cravat and then proceeded to knead the back of his neck three times, as he did every time he attempted to fib. Drake wasn't fooling Diana. In the months leading up to Minerva's debut Season, Diana had been certain she'd seen the frequent glimmers of interest in Drake's eyes as Minerva transformed right before everyone, from country girl to an elegant lady of the *ton*. Diana had hoped Drake would finally come to his senses and take up Minerva's challenge. Not that she believed Drake capable of defeating her sister; however, Diana suspected Minerva would gracefully lose to a gentleman that would be caring and loyal.

It was obvious to Diana that they held an affection for one another, yet as each Season passed, Minerva became more and more determined not to marry, and Drake purposefully distanced himself further from her. Diana's efforts to devise a covert plan in which the two would come to their senses had failed miserably. Minerva was adept at anticipating her every move. An image of the Beast of Chestwick flashed before her—mayhap she could recruit the aid of the brilliant strategist.

The drawing room door swung open, and the Beast himself appeared. All thoughts of her sister and Drake vanished as a clean-shaven Lord Chestwick approached. A fine, white scar slashed down his cheek and along his jawline. Diana swallowed a lump that had formed in her throat. The marring of his features didn't detract from the man's impressive looks. All Diana saw were his unique dual-color eyes that were bright in contrast to this dark-colored jacket.

Diana's gaze remained locked on his as he marched across the room to stand before her. He acknowledged the greetings of her family with the barest of nods. Her heart raced. Why, out of all the gentlemen of her acquaintance, did Randal garner such visceral reactions from her?

Drake rose, and Diana said, "Lord Chestwick, may I introduce you to our neighbor, Lord Drake."

Lord Chestwick again acknowledged his guest with a minimalist nod. "Since I don't recall having met you previously, I'll assume you attended Eton rather than Harrow."

Drake, easily the most congenial of their set, stiffened and replied,

"You are correct. I attended Eton along with Kent and Cunningham."

Diana searched the room for Minerva, hoping she might interject and ease the tension in the room. Rather than locating Minerva, Diana's gaze fell upon Isadora—who sadly shook her head and jutted her chin toward the door. Diana's heart sank. Minerva had fled again. Without the aid of her eldest sister, Diana sought out Isadora's assistance. Her sister acknowledged Diana's plea with a smile, squared her shoulders, and linked her arm with Lord Cunningham to steer him over to their small group.

Diana clasped her hands tightly in her lap. She was aware Lord Chestwick's gaze was trained back on her. He had made it abundantly clear yesterday that he did not care for guests, and yet she was about to make more introductions.

Isadora and Cunningham stepped into the empty space next to Drake. Diana cleared her throat. "Lord Chestwick, may I also introduce to you my dear sister Lady Isadora and the esteemed Lord Cunningham, who also resides close by."

Lord Chestwick's features were calm and relaxed, but a tick in his jaw was a sign he was not at all pleased with her family and friends' uninvited descent upon Chestwick Hall.

"Lord Cunningham. Lady Isadora, a pleasure. Lady Diana, I would like to speak to you…" Lord Chestwick glanced about those standing and added, "In private."

Before she could give the others a signal to leave, Lord Chestwick scooped her up into his arms like had the day before and carried her out of the room.

"You cannot just pick me up any time you wish! Where are you taking me?"

"Back to your chambers where you are supposed to be resting and recovering."

"My chambers! You cannot be serious."

"I am."

"But what about the others?"

"Once I see you settled, I shall dispatch them and inform them not to return. They can confirm you are alive and well at Malbury Manor in three days hence."

She lifted her hand to his cheek, her little finger resting along the slightly raised skin. "Why is your solitude so important?" When he didn't flinch or brush off her touch, she gently turned his face toward her.

He stopped and looked at her directly, his mouth opened to answer. Diana dropped her gaze to his lips.

When he sealed his lips into a tight line, she grinned and said, "I promise not to laugh if you tell me." The corner of his mouth twitched.

"If I answer your query—will you promise you shall stay abed for the remainder of your stay."

Diana rubbed her thumb along his strong jawline. It would be a challenge to linger in her chambers when she desperately wanted to be in the library. Diana peered up at Lord Chestwick. "I promise."

"It is not solitude I seek. It is simply a matter of safeguarding oneself."

What could the Beast of Chestwick possibly be afraid of? She lowered her hand from his face and placed it against his chest. "From what?"

"I agreed to provide you an answer to your question, not explain the logic behind my decision to keep others at bay."

Riddles! The man was akin to his papa, always speaking in double entendre. Had she not hoped to find a man who shared her love of riddles? Transfixed by Lord Chestwick's hazel eyes, Diana remained mute.

Lord Chestwick arched a brow. "No bargaining. No arguments?"

"I realize it is unfair of me to expect you to confide in me. I shall have to wait until I have gained your trust. Trust I sense you rarely grant."

He's gaze bore into her, but like before, he remained silent, leaving her guessing as to what his thoughts could be. After a moment, he shook his head and resumed marching her back to her room.

Safely tucked against his chest, she let her mind wander back to the problem of Minerva and Drake. With the door to her chambers in sight, Diana gathered her courage to seek out her host's assistance. "Lord Chestwick..."

"Randal. You should call me Randal."

"Very well, Randal." His name rolled off her tongue as if she'd spoken it a thousand times before. "If I am to retire to my chambers for the remainder of my stay, I hope the edict doesn't also extend to my sister Minerva."

"I see no reason why it should."

"Grand. I believe she is hiding in my rooms now. If Minerva returned with you to the library, my reputation should remain intact and, she is very skilled at dispatching unwanted guests."

"I should hope you had more faith in my abilities to dispatch a few guests."

He wasn't the scary beast gossips made him out to be, and her family was not easily ordered about. "You have been abroad for many years. You know little of my family and our neighbors. Trust me, you shall need Minerva's help."

He stopped in front of her chamber door. "Was it not you who mere moments ago hypothesized that I rarely trust others?"

"Aye, but I assure you—you can trust me." Diana searched his features. His austere appearance softened, and a flicker of emotion she could not pinpoint flashed briefly in his eyes. Randal was an enigma. Before she took her leave of Chestwick Hall, she vowed to gain the man's trust and unmask the Beast of Chestwick.

Randal chuckled. "I'd be dead if I believed every person who claimed themselves trustworthy." He bent and waited for her to open the door.

Hand on the latch, Diana replied, "Your life is no longer in danger. You are safe here." The full hearty rumble from Randal's chest caught her off guard. "What is so amusing?"

"Nothing." He shook his head. "Please open the door."

Diana searched the man's face once more. Nothing. His features revealed nothing of his thoughts. Frustrated, she unlatched the door and pushed it open. Minera was pacing in front of the window with her hands clasped behind her back and muttering to herself.

Minerva swiveled, and her brows slashed into a fierce frown. "Diana, is your ankle worse?"

Randal strode over to the large bed and placed her upon the soft mattress. Diana shimmied back to sit up against the headboard. "No, my ankle is fine."

Her sister shoved Randal to the side and began arranging pillows to elevate her injured ankle. Minerva blocked her view of Randal, which also meant he couldn't see Diana flinch every time her sister moved her ankle. While she was in his arms, she had barely noticed the pain, but the dreadful throbbing had returned.

Minerva swiveled and glared at their host.

Randal took a step away from the bed and toward the door. "I believe I shall take my leave now."

Diana peered around her sister. "Mayhap, you could escort Minerva back to the library."

"Absolutely not." Minerva turned her attention to Diana. "I shall remain here with you."

"I agree. Lady Minerva can tend to you while I deal with the uninvited guests under my roof." Randal left her chambers without another word.

Diana reached for Minerva's hand and squeezed. "He'll need your help."

"Aye—he will." Minerva's lips slowly curved into a smile. "I'll rescue him after you share with me the blasted riddle that has landed us in this mess."

The warmth of her sister's love and understanding enveloped Diana. How could she ever repay her sister's kindness?

CHAPTER TEN

WITHOUT DIANA IN his arms, a void settled in Randal's chest. The merriment that had filtered through the halls earlier was eerily absent, bringing thoughts of his mama to the forefront of Randal's mind. He missed his mama's infectious laughter and her unwavering positivity. Until Diana's arrival, he had forgotten how fortunate he was to have inherited Chestwick Hall. The estate was full of potential, and with a little bit of effort on his part, Randal could restore it to its former glory—to once again be a haven for him and his family.

With his hand on the latch of the library door, Randal breathed in and steeled himself to face his neighbors and Diana's family on the other side. He didn't know these people, and they knew nothing of him. He wasn't ready to infiltrate the intimate circle of the *ton*. He needed time to adjust.

Randal was caught entirely by surprise when he opened the door to find Isadora and her brother Greg quietly playing chess by the fire, while Kent, Drake, and Cunningham were engaged in a serious game of cards near the window. Not one of them paid any mind to the hundreds of books that surrounded them. Volumes that Diana was eager to discover the contents of.

Kent placed his cards face down on the table in front of him. "Chestwick, you have returned." Diana's brother motioned to the empty chair to his right. "Care to join us? Commerce is the game today."

Randal controlled the spark of ire at being invited to partake in an activity being held in his own home. If he trounced them a round or two, perhaps his guests would grow bored and willingly leave of their own accord. He nodded, and the ever-present footman, whose name escaped Randal but most likely was known by Diana, pulled the chair out for him. Why could he not block the woman from his every thought? Seated at the table, Randal waited for the current round to be completed.

Rather than continuing the game, Drake gathered the cards from the others and began to deftly shuffle them. "For years, we've been wanting to see the interior of Chestwick Hall. It is as impressive as Diana claimed."

How had his papa kept the neighbors at bay all these years, yet, in the span a day, he had failed and been invaded, and the enemy had made themselves at home?

Drake dealt three cards to each player before revealing the three-card window.

Randal noted the absence of a pool. "What is at stake?"

Kent answered, "Fence repairs."

Randal frowned.

Kent continued, "We don't play for money amongst family and friends."

Cunningham elaborated, "The loser is responsible for the fence repairs along our property lines. Drake has yet to win and has been reigning king of overseeing to the task. What is it now, three years straight?"

Drake chuckled. "Better fence repairs than ditch maintenance."

Kent eyed Randal. "We should play for that next."

He hadn't played idle card games in years. All eyes were on him.

Kent leaned over and whispered, "Eldest is to act first."

Arranging and rearranging his cards, he recalled the aim was to form a hand with the highest combination. Three of a kind was the goal. With two tens, a mid-range pair, he was not likely to win, however the window contained a knave. Mathematically calculating the odds, Randal traded his two of hearts for the knave of spades, giving him the possibility of making a sequence.

Next to act was Drake. He glanced at his cards and knocked, indicating he was already happy with his hand. Drake looked over at Kent and said, "Next season, you'll not stop me from finishing Mansville and his set off."

Isadora and Greg joined them at the card table flanking their brother, Kent. Footmen produced chairs for them both, and Kent shifted his own seat to allow his siblings to join in the conversation.

Isadora turned to face Drake on her right. "Mansville's luck will run out in due time. No need to place Minerva in further peril."

"Your sister is in danger?" Randal directed his question to Kent.

Kent sighed, "In Minerva's first Season, she declared she would marry the first gentleman who could defeat her in a game of chess. Upon hearing the challenge, Mansville, the blasted peacock, placed a wager at Brooks's, claiming that he'd not only win Minerva's hand in marriage, but he would do so in less than twenty moves."

Greg glanced at Drake and then added, "Minerva learned of the wager and set out to defeat Mansville in as few possible moves. When she trounced the man in twenty-two moves, Mansville was outraged, claimed she was a cheat. However, the game had been played out under Lady Humbolt's watchful gaze. Humbolt has since banned Mansville from attending a number of social events, which has only increased the man's ire."

No one was paying any attention to the game, and Isadora gave each of the men a scolding stare. "It wasn't Lady Humbolt's support of Minverva these past three Seasons that has spurred Mansville's attempts to foil Minerva's future, it is the actions of each of you." Her gaze moved from one gentleman to the next and ultimately landed on her eldest brother, Kent. "Because of you fools, not one gentleman dared to even hint at entertaining the idea of playing Minerva for her hand this past Season." Pinning her brother Kent with a look that would have sent his troops scurrying to the hills, Isadora added, "You shall end up responsible for the three of us. Diana nor I shall marry before Minerva."

Everyone jumped in their seats as Minerva's voice wafted across the room. "Nonsense. Diana and you shall marry as soon as you have found a man worthy of your love. I shall see to it."

Gregory jumped up from his seat and offered it to Minerva.

Minerva took her seat and held out her hand. Without a word, Kent and the others handed over their cards to her. She waited for him to do the same.

Curious as what she would do if he refused, he studied her features. The slight arch of her brow had him handing over his cards, but before she could take them, he asked, "What about the fence repairs?"

She looked at him directly and said, "I'm quite certain Lord Drake shall volunteer as he does every year."

"Volunteer?"

Cunningham answered, "It is the only round Drake consistently loses every year."

Drake's cheeks flooded red, his gaze flickering over to Minerva, but she ignored him entirely.

Minerva handed the cards to her sister, and Isadora shuffled the deck in an artful display, fanning the cards and intermingling them effortlessly. Isadora asked, "What shall we play for today, sister?"

None of the gentleman uttered a sound. Randal noted the look of trepidation on each of their faces as they waited for Minerva to answer.

Diana's eldest sister was in full command. Minerva tapped her finger over her lips. Drake's gaze focused on the woman, which drew a frown from Kent. The undercurrents were strong, but he didn't know them well enough to fully understand all the intricacies and implications of their body language.

Minerva's gaze fell upon him. "The honor of choosing the rest of the afternoon's entertainment."

Drake spoke, "Grand. With Chestwick, we have a four-to-one advantage."

Isadora passed the deck back to Minerva, who dealt the cards. Once again, all eyes fell upon him. "Should you win, Lady Minerva, what would your choice of entertainment be?"

Drake mumbled, "Not chess."

In a clear voice, she asked, "If circumstances were different, I would not hesitate to partake in a game of chess. However, should I win at Commerce, I believe an afternoon of charades would be highly entertaining."

Kent groaned, "Not charades."

Drake straightened in his chair and flickered his gaze between Minerva and Randal. "Let's get on with the game."

They each took turns discarding and rearranging their hands. Minerva was the first to knock, indicating she was satisfied with her hand. Randal glanced down at the pair of eights; he hoped no one else held the last eight of clubs he needed to ensure a win. When Isadora flipped over the card he so desperately needed and added it to the window, he had never been so glad to be the eldest in the room.

He slowed his nerves and switched out his card. His hand complete, he knocked, ending the round. Everyone revealed their hands. Cunningham, Kent, and Isadora all revealed pairs, but Drake had a diamond flush, and Minerva held an ace-high sequence. Only a tricon would have been Minerva, and he held one with eights. Drake's frustration at losing was evident, but Randal wasn't sure if it was due to losing to him or having been bested by Minerva.

Isadora stared at the cards laid out. "Do you see what I see?" The young woman looked up at him, then over to her brother. "Minerva lost."

While everyone else was looking in disbelief at the cards laid out upon the table, Minerva gave him a wink. The only other person to catch the mischievous look was Drake, who pushed away from the table and stood. "Chestwick, I assume it is your wish for all of us to leave you in peace. My thanks for your hospitality, and please pass my wishes on to Lady Diana for a speedy recovery."

Isadora was the next to rise from the card table. She placed a kiss upon Minerva's cheek. "I shall return on the morrow."

"We *all* shall, to check upon Diana." Kent stood and turned to speak to his brother Greg who was still studying the cards upon the table.

Randal stood, intending to inform Kent and the others that they would not be granted entrance again, but the sadness in Minerva's gaze trained on Drake's back tugged on his heart, and for the first time in a very long time, he altered his decision.

He tipped his head in both Cunningham and Kent's direction as they moved to leave and gave Isadora a smile as she bobbed a quick curtsy and rushed to follow her brother out the door.

Greg spread out the discarded pile and said, "You knocked two full turns before Chestwick, the probability of you winning was still in your favor."

"My plan had naught to do with Lord Chestwick. Diana made me promise to dispatch the others as quickly and economically as possible, and I kept my word."

He did appreciate Minerva's effective methods. But he didn't care to see the pain in the woman's eyes when Drake had all but given her the cut direct when he failed to bid Minerva farewell. Unrequited love was difficult to witness.

Minerva stood and excused herself, claiming a walk in the gardens in the fresh air would be nice. Greg silently accompanied his sister out the terrace doors. A knot twisted in his stomach. The misty quality of Minerva's eyes as she left the room reminded him of the day his mama summoned him to her chambers and informed him that there was no healing from her ailment. He couldn't prevent his mama's death, but mayhap he could help Minerva.

In order to accomplish such a feat, he would need to gain as much insight as possible into Minerva's predicament. Diana. She would be able to provide him with the intel he required. He strode to the door and paused—what was he doing, formulating excuses to spend more time with Diana?

Randal retraced his steps back to the table and glanced down at the playing cards lain askew. *Astonishing.* The Malburys were blessed with sharp minds. It was no small feat to perform the complex calculation with all the cards revealed, let alone while during play. Diana was right. Minerva was an excellent strategist.

As Randal knew all too well, there were times when skillful tacticians got lost in their own schemes. Exiting the library, Randal headed directly back to Diana's chambers. With each step he took, he attempted to convince himself his motives were purely for Minerva's benefit. But that was a lie—he was seeking out Diana's company purely to relieve himself of the hollow feeling that had engulfed him since he had left her side.

CHAPTER ELEVEN

THE METHODICAL HEAVY booted footsteps that were quickly becoming familiar were getting louder. Diana gathered the slew of papers scattered over the bed. She wasn't quick enough before the door to her bed chambers swung open. "Randal! You are supposed to scratch at the door and wait for my command to enter. What if I hadn't been decent?"

"It is in the middle of the day—why wouldn't you be decent?"

Diana blinked at her host. Was he teasing her? There had been a lightness to his tone she'd never heard before. He must have enjoyed spending time with her family and neighbors. They were, for the majority of the time, rather fun.

"Where is Minerva?"

"Out for a walk in the gardens with your brother."

"You can't be in here."

"My house, my rules." He pointed to the stack of parchment tightly gripped in her hands. "What have you there?"

"Notes I've compiled."

He rested his hip against the bed and crossed his arms over his chest. "Attempting to solve my papa's puzzle without the aid of the library or me?"

"I still do not recall asking for your assistance. Access to the library, however, would be helpful."

He pushed off the bed and walked over to the window. "How long has Minerva been in love with Drake?"

"What makes you believe my sister is in love with Lord Drake?"

"Am I wrong—is she not in love with the man?"

"Rather than us continuing to answer each other's questions with a question—a game I play quite often with my siblings—I propose for each answer I provide, I'm granted an hour in the library."

"And for each answer I provide, what will you grant me?"

"What is it you want?"

He ceased pacing and swiveled to face her. Her breath caught at the sight of his furrowed brow and thinned lips. She had either angered the man, or he was appalled at her question.

"What are you willing to give?"

Blast the man. He, too, was quite skilled at the game. "It is not a question of what I'm willing to concede, but what do I possess that is of interest to you?"

He smiled and walked back to stand next to the bed. "Do you really want to find out?"

She laid the papers down upon the bed and then clasped her hands in her lap. Smiling, she looked up and said, "I do."

"You desire to gain access to the library, and I want…" He raked a hand through his hair.

She wasn't a mind reader, but she recognized the flare of yearning in his eyes. She'd witnessed it numerous times when her papa gazed at other women and on the rare occasions when Lord Drake believed Minerva unaware of his presence. It was the look she had avoided all Season but had only a few hours ago fantasized about seeing it in Randal's hazel eyes. She bit down on her lower lip, a habit she'd developed to prevent her from speaking.

Randal sank down to the bed and cupped her face. "I want you."

"If it is me that you want, why were you inquiring about Minerva?"

He dropped his hands from her face. "This afternoon in the library, your sister exhibited a skill I'd never witnessed before."

"The ability to maneuver people like chess pieces."

Randal frowned. "We are each responsible for our own actions. No one forced Lord Drake or the others to take their leave."

"Aye, that is true, but Minerva is exceptionally skilled in predicting the reactions of others."

"She said she acted out of a promise to you."

"Oh, did she?" Diana crossed her arms over her chest and huffed. "Well, that promise cost me three months' worth of pin money."

"Why would you agree to such an arrangement?"

She rolled her eyes and said, "It was the only way I could get her to enter a room she knew Drake occupied. And while you do not care, it *is* important for you to build a rapport with those gentlemen who share a border with your estate."

"I agree." He drummed his fingers over his thigh—a rather muscular thigh that she had ran her hand over the other day. She should have lingered over him in her examination, then she wouldn't be plagued with curiosity that was driving her to distraction. Giving into temptation, she uncrossed her arms and placed a hand over his to still his movements.

Randal's gaze fell upon their hands and then back up to her eyes. "Minerva is not the only one in your family who is able to anticipate and coordinate the action of others." He rubbed his thumb back and forth along the width of her wrist. "Do you know what occurred for your sister to have such a dislike of Drake's company?"

"I do, but I'm at a loss as to how to repair the damage Drake caused with his callous comments."

His soothing caress ceased. "What did he say?" A flush appeared across the bridge of his nose and on the tops of his cheeks. Diana's heart cinched. The ache was unfamiliar. Was it jealousy or self-disappointment that she may yield and break her promise not to fall in love before Minerva married?

Taking a deep breath, she sighed and said, "It is a very long story."

"I'm in no hurry to leave."

"Very well. At the end of last summer, Benedict, Drake, and Cunningham were all in our papa's study. Minerva and I were passing by to fetch books from the library. We stopped when we overheard the three of them discussing my debut season. Benedict claimed he was at a loss as to how to protect all three of us. Cunningham laughingly suggested Drake should marry Minerva. Benedict laughed and made a statement that as his best friend, Drake would never do such a thing. Drake joined in the laughter and professed he had absolutely no interest in marrying Minerva and that the idea gave him hives. Minerva never said anything, but from that night forth, she has avoided Drake, and he, the fool, has done nothing to repair the special bond they had shared since we were children. I believed Drake sincerely cared and loved Minerva. But I was wrong."

"Do you think Drake would act upon jealousy? What if he believed there was a chance of losing her to another? Do you believe he may act upon his true feelings?"

"You have spent very little time with them. What occurred this afternoon that gives you the impression Drake loves Minerva?"

"Nothing specific…at least not quantifiable occurred, but I trust you and your instincts. I doubt you are wrong about the situation. And while I sensed Minerva's feeling for Drake, he did a remarkable job of hiding his feelings for her this afternoon. I assume that was because your brothers were present."

"How would we make Drake jealous?"

"Perhaps if Drake believed I was entertaining the idea of engaging in a game of chess…"

"If you won, would you wed Minerva?"

"I witnessed your sister's fine mathematical mind this afternoon, despite her loss to me. While I'm a skilled strategist on the battlefield,

I'm not confident that I would be able to outwit your sister in a game of chess."

A near-silent thump had Diana scanning the room. Minerva, with her back leaned up against the door jam, arms crossed, and with a lopsided smile, said, "There is no doubt in my mind you would lose."

Randal leapt off the bed and placed his hands firmly behind him. His lips were twisted into a smirk, but as he turned to face her sister, they thinned into a firm line. He might attempt to fool others into believing he was a surly soul, but Diana had been privy to brief glimpses into his sweet nature.

He strode across the room, headed directly for the door. Minerva quickly stepped out of the threshold into Diana's chambers. With a curt nod, he waltzed past and disappeared down the corridor.

Minerva flopped onto the bed. "You know how scandalous it is to have an eligible gentleman alone in your chambers. I'm going to pretend I did not witness the pair of you holding hands."

"How long have you been eavesdropping?" Diana asked.

"I made no secret of my approach. It's not my fault you two were so engrossed in each other you didn't hear me." Minerva settled herself on the bed next to Diana. "Life is not like a Shakespearean play, unfortunately. Drake would not care a wit if I was to marry Chestwick or even one of Mansville's nefarious cronies."

"That is not true," Diana said, reaching for her sister's hand. "And Benedict would never let that wretched Mansville nor any of his associates marry you."

"I'll not ruin Isadora or your chances for a happy marriage. Mayhap I'll purposefully lose to the next man who sits across a chessboard from me."

"Do you still love Drake?"

"Aye."

"Then we should seriously consider Randal's plan."

"Randal?"

"He asked me to refer to him by his given name."

"Just because a gentleman gives you leave to do something doesn't mean you must. Regardless, do you have feelings of the romantic sort for Chestwick?"

"I've only known him for two days, but I feel as if I've known him for longer due to having heard so many stories about him from his papa. But he's not exactly the man I had pictured in my mind. He is more."

Both stared up at the ceiling, lost in thought. An uneasy feeling rolled through Diana as she pictured Randal playing a game of chess with Minerva. What if the inconceivable occurred and Minerva didn't win? Would she be forced to keep her word and marry him?

CHAPTER TWELVE

THE BREAKFAST ROOM was filled with chatter by Diana and her two siblings. Peering over the edge of his copy of the *Daily Gazette*, Randal caught Diana's beautiful smile. She had limericks and verses of poetry running through his mind, which was a wonderful change from battlefield orders and stratagems that had occupied his thoughts for far too many years.

The sound of booted footsteps heralded the arrival of Kent and Drake, who, without invitation, entered and gave Randal the briefest of nods as they made their way over to the sideboard.

Randal crisply folded and lowered the paper, placing it front of the empty seat next to him. He noted the conspiratorial looks between Diana and Minerva.

Minerva said, "Brother, it is customary for you to greet our host."

Kent said, "A good morn to you, Chestwick." He set his plate on the table and settled into the chair next to Minerva, who asked, "Did you not already break your fast before arriving?"

Kent answered, "No, Drake arrived early and demanded we set out as soon as I was dressed."

Drake sat next to Diana. "How is your injury faring?"

Greg answered, "Diana is recovering remarkably well. We should be able to return home tomorrow…that is if she continues to rest and refrain from attempting to walk."

The level of familiarity and comradery amongst them reminded Randal of nights spent around a campfire discussing the next day's maneuvers with his men. He missed his men. He missed the feeling of being in charge. Since Diana entered his universe, he was no longer the ruler of his own thoughts. The woman plagued his mind, and his body ached to be near her constantly. He glanced at his guests that filled every seat at the ostentatious breakfast table. It was obvious that his home had been seized, and he needed to regain control. Except his decision to be rid of his guests instantly fled as he gaze fell upon Diana.

The woman who was responsible for all his internal turmoil groaned, "I detest being carried about." Diana sent a pleading look over at Minerva to no avail, for Minerva's head was bent as she focused on smearing jam upon her toast. She was clearly avoiding all eye contact with the man seated opposite her.

Kent swallowed and waved his fork in the air toward their brother. "Until Greg says you can place weight upon that foot, you shall either remain in your chambers or firmly seated upon a chaise in the library."

Minerva glared at her brother. "Need I remind you this is not your home."

Drake muttered, "Nor are you the lady of this monstrosity."

The barb caused both Diana and Minerva to inhale sharply and Randal to stand. The loud scraping of his chair sent all eyes his way. "I believe it is time we all adjourn to the library." He walked over to Diana, bent, and picked her up.

Wide-eyed and speechless, Diana simply wrapped one arm around the back of his neck and peered up at him.

Adjusting his hold, bringing Diana closer, he spoke over his shoulder. "Lady Minerva would you please do me the honor of leading the way." He let Minerva proceed him, and stepped forward, preventing Drake from following. Randal pierced his guest with a glare that had had many a man flee the battlefield. Rather than taking a step back, Drake merely stood and returned Randal's steeling stare.

Once they were past the threshold and a few feet away from Drake, Diana whispered, "Why are you allowing me to join you and the others today?"

"I shall need you to keep Drake occupied while I speak with your sister to see if she is willing to participate in our plan to bring Drake up to scratch."

"You are going to engage Minerva in a game of chess?"

"Was that not our plan?" Randal asked.

"No, that was your terrible idea, although I do believe it would work."

Diana believed him capable of defeating her sister. Her unquestioning faith and belief in him was unsettling.

Diana sighed. "I do wish to see Minerva happy again. I shall distract Drake. But I warn you, Minerva is terrible at feigning any reactions, so in order for Drake to truly believe this farce, you will have to be charming."

What retort would turn her frown into a smile? "I'm always charming."

"You are no prince but a beast."

He faked surprise. "A beast?"

"Aye. Ordering everyone about."

He jostled her a little and whispered, "And carry my victims about." The grin on Diana's face created yet another new experience for him.

Minerva opened the door to the library, and Randal waited for her to enter before putting a barrier between Diana's sister and Drake.

He deposited Diana on the chaise lounge. He turned and came face to face with Drake, who shot daggers at him. Randal sidestepped the man, and Drake sank down into the seat next to Diana. He glanced down at Diana, who gave him a wink. He'd never had a co-conspirator before, and it was nice not to feel all alone—a feeling he'd not had since his mama's death.

He savored the feeling as he made his way over to Minerva, who was standing by the windows alone.

Minerva didn't miss a beat. As soon as he was next to her, she asked, "Diana shared with me your preposterous theorem that jealousy would prompt Lord Drake to offer for my hand." She never took her eyes away from the garden.

"Do you not wish to marry Lord Drake?"

"It is he who does not wish to marry me."

"Doubtful." Randal peered into the window reflection and caught the real subject matter that held Minerva's interest. It wasn't his immaculately maintained garden; it was Drake's image. "I applaud your devilishly ingenious scheme. Your declaration to marry only the man who defeats you in chess ensured it was *you* who would choose your partner for life. You are a skilled strategist, and I'm certain you are fully aware of your abilities and believe without a doubt you would have no issue defeating any opponent, thus if you were to lose, it would be because you wish it so, not due to a man outwitting you. Am I wrong?"

"Aye, you are mistaken. When I play, I play to win no matter who my opponent is." She turned to face him. "Is it unreasonable to want to spend the rest of my days with a gentleman who is of similar intellect? Someone I may converse with, and not simply the first gentleman who gained enough courage to ask for my hand."

"No, it is not." Intellect had been one of his own requirements for his future countess. "What would you say if I proposed we played a game of chess?"

"I'd refuse."

"Why?"

"Because you do not wish to marry me."

"Truth be told, I'm not yet ready to marry," he said.

She studied him closely. "That may be the case; however, I also know Drake. I know him well, and jealous or not, he would never offer to marry me."

He had to change tactics. Perhaps if he placed her on the defensive, he might get his way.

"Do you fear I may defeat you?"

"Ha. I highly doubt soldiers carry about with them a chess set. When was the last time you even played?"

"I believe I was twelve." He hadn't played with wooden pieces, but his chess pieces had been of the human variety. "If you believe you can easily defeat me, what is the harm? It will afford you an excuse to ignore Drake."

He did not take his gaze away from her as she pondered over his argument. He heard someone approaching from behind. "Lady Minerva, you best makeyour decision."

Clapping a hand on Randal's shoulder, Drake asked, "What are the two of you whispering about?"

Minerva answered loudly enough for all to hear, "Lord Chestwick would like to play a game of chess, and I was explaining to him the risks of doing so."

"Having just returned from the Continent, I wasn't aware you were in a rush to marry."

"To wed was the primary reason I returned to England. Duty to the title and all." Randal smiled at Minerva. "If I were to win, Minerva would be saving me from having to endure the trials of a Season."

"Minerva, you cannot possibly be considering playing Chestwick."

"Why not?"

"You have known him for all of what? Two days?"

"What does it matter if I've known my opponent for days or years?"

Drake turned to the eldest Malbury. "Kent, are you going to allow this nonsense to proceed?"

Kent looked at Minerva. "Do you wish to play Chestwick?"

Minerva glanced at Diana, who nodded. What was the look about?

Minerva turned to face Randal. "Let us be clear upon the terms."

Randal nodded. "I win, I have your hand in marriage. If you win…"

Minerva leaned in to speak directly into his ear so Drake and none of the others could hear. "Agreed, if you win, we shall marry; however, if I win, you, Lord Chestwick, will marry Diana by summer's end."

Randal leaned back and frowned. He glanced at Kent, who had a worried look. "Why would I agree to such terms."

The idea of marrying Diana appealed to him, but to admit it… However, he hardly knew her.

"My terms are non-negotiable. Do you accept?"

Minerva's steady gaze had a trickling of unease rolling down his back. She was playing to win.

He turned back to glance at Diana. The frown and uncertainty told him she was not aware of her sister's scheme. He wouldn't want his future to be dictated by another. He leaned in close to Minerva. "Does Diana know of your terms?"

"Nay."

He winged his arm and pulled her away from Drake and the others and toward the chess board. "Would you wish for another to dictate who is to be your husband?"

Minerva's steps faltered. "Nay."

"What do you say if we modify the terms slightly—should you win, I shall afford Diana full unrestricted access to the library at Chestwick Hall."

Minerva's eyebrow arched. "And…"

"And?"

"My lord, I'm not blind, nor am I a dolt. You never let Diana out of view. Even now, you position yourself in order to keep her in your peripheral line of view." Minerva took a half step forward to block his view and punctuate her statement. "Whether you wish to acknowledge it or not, you are drawn to my sister." She pinned him with a stare.

He caved. "I shall agree to your terms—I win, we shall marry. You win, and I shall marry your sister."

Chapter Thirteen

Balling the soft cotton material of her skirts in her hand, Diana willed Minerva to turn around. The lines in Randal's forehead only deepened as he peered down at Minerva. What could they be discussing? The serious slash of Randal's eyebrows had Diana staring at the man. If he believed he'd intimidate Minerva, the man was in for a shock—the horrid moniker of Ice Queen was unfortunately all too true. Nothing aside from Drake could ruffle Minera's feathers. She shifted her weight to gain a better view of Randal.

"Sister, mine. If you lean any further, you shall injure yourself once more." Greg pulled his chair closer. "It doesn't appear Chestwick is all too impressed with Minerva's demands should she win."

"What do you think she is bargaining for this time?"

"I fear to guess." Greg stretched out his legs and crossed them at the ankles.

Randal held out the chair for Minerva and turned to take his seat. He stopped briefly to stand toe-to-toe with Drake. Neither man appeared pleased with the other. Drake was the first to act, producing what Diana knew was an artificial upward turn of the lips into a smile that she was beginning to resent.

Diana righted her posture and asked, "Why is it frowned upon to have a friend marry a sister?"

Solemn faced, Greg replied, "Our dear old brother knows every dark secret Drake possesses. Every single one, and I can attest they are not saints."

"Neither are you."

"Aye, but…this is not a topic for your ears."

It was asinine for men to believe women didn't talk, but she was in no mood to spar with Gregory. Diana returned her gaze back to her sister, who was busy assembling her pieces. Randal, on the other hand, was seated and relaxed in his chair with his arms crossed against his chest and appeared to be studying both Minerva and the board before him. A bolt of anger hit her. What had she been thinking? Minerva was correct—jealousy would not provoke Drake into a proposal, but the irrational emotion could very well result in both Drake and Chestwick standing in an empty field at dawn.

Shooing her morbid thoughts from her mind, Diana focused on the more pleasant activity of admiring Randal's profile. For years she had wondered what the man in the portraits would be like in real life. From her observations, none of the painters had accurately captured Randal's unique ability to swiftly adapt to his surroundings.

Drake moved to stand between the chess opponents, slightly blocking Diana's view of Randal, the chessboard, and its pieces. The material of Drake's jacket was stretched taut across his back. She leaned toward her brother, but her view remained hindered. "Do you agree with Kent—that Drake would be a terrible match for Minerva?"

"My opinion matters not."

"Of course your opinion counts. If it didn't, why would I have bothered to ask?"

Greg glanced at her and frowned. "Even if I did disagree with Kent's belief, there is naught we could do."

"Ah, but what if…"

Greg raised a hand to stop her from continuing. "I know that look, and I want no part in your scheme."

Drake moved to stand behind Randal, capturing Diana's attention.

Mayhap their plan would work. Drake's inability to remain in one place was in stark contrast to his normal laissez-faire attitude when Minerva was present.

Diana lowered her gaze to Randal. His features relaxed as he chatted with Minerva as he prepared his pieces on the board. Minerva gave him her full attention, ignoring Drake with ease. It appeared neither Minerva nor Randal was in any rush for the game to begin. Randal picked up another piece and twirled it between his thumb and forefinger. His full lips twisted into a smile as he spoke.

She was too far away to hear Randal's short tale, but she noticed Drake rolled his eyes each time Minerva smiled or laughed. With a clear view of Minerva, Drake appeared more relaxed and even seemed to be enjoying Randal's musings. The stubborn fool was no longer exhibiting any signs of jealousy. Randal needed to cease entertaining them both and start wooing her sister. Minerva needed to be the recipient of those devilishly wicked smiles that made Diana's mind go blank.

Greg's warm voice intruded Diana's thoughts. "While they play, shall we make most of the distraction and work on those riddles you are determined to solve."

How was she to concentrate on the riddles when Randal was seated opposite Minerva, playing potentially for her hand? But Greg was right; she should make the most of her time in the library before Randal changed his mind.

"My notes are in my chamber."

"Shall I go fetch them for you?"

"If you don't mind. I believe I left them on the table next to the window."

"I'll have Kent come keep you company." Greg stood.

"Must you?"

Her brother placed a hand on her shoulder. "I don't know what occurred for you and Minerva to dislike our brother so, but he only wants the best for you both."

"Pfft." She shrugged, dislodging Greg's hand, and crossed her arms over her chest. She glanced up at her brother. "All Kent cares about is proving to Papa he is worthy of the title."

"A little harsh, sister." He left her side.

Harsh—the truth often was.

She sighed. Her gaze stopped at the sight of Randal smirking and Drake frowning at the chessboard. Diana stretched her neck in hopes of garnering a better glimpse of the board.

"I believe Minerva is finally playing a worthy opponent?"

"Hmph." She glared at Kent. "We both know that the only way Minerva loses is if she wishes it so."

Kent bent and placed an arm under her knees and about her back. "Let's relocate to gain a better view, shall we?"

Her brother picked her up, and she caught Randal scowling at her. She smiled, and oddly his lips didn't twitch at the corners like she had become accustomed to seeing. Was he angry with her? As they approached, Randal stood and signaled to the nearest footman to assist him with moving a rather large chair next to the chessboard.

Kent said, "Good lord, Drake, stop staring at the blasted pieces and come help bring over a footrest for Diana."

Drake looked about dazed and moved to assist in arranging furniture to allow her a better view. Randal had placed the chair to face him directly. How was she to continue her covert assessment of him if he was directly in front of her? She liked watching him attempt to control his features and failing to hide his thoughts.

Settled, Diana asked, "Whose turn is it?"

Drake answered, "Minerva's."

Kent shifted slightly closer to Minerva now that he stood in between them. "Interesting. Interesting indeed."

Diana studied the board. She hadn't even considered the possibility of a stalemate, whereby neither was declared a winner, until now. Is that what the pair had been discussing earlier? What would occur if a tie was to be declared? Minerva had positioned her pawns potentially where they may all be blocked. Diana was no chess master, but she had played her fair share of games against her brilliant sister to recognize Minerva was not employing her normal strategy of win in as few moves as possible.

She peered up at Randal, who was watching her, not the board and not his opponent. A warmth spread through her as his eyes twinkled at her, and his lips curved into a smile. He was rather dashing when he smiled.

Drake leaned his hip against the side of Randal's chair. "What are you waiting for Minerva? There is only one rational move for you to make?"

Minerva raised her chin and met Drake's disgruntled features. "Pray tell, what do you have at stake that has you interested in the outcome of this game? Have you placed yet another idiotic wager?"

Kent asked, "What do you know of wagers and such?"

Minerva's eyes never left Drake, who was rubbing his wrists. A tell he developed as a child that he was nervous or hiding something. Despite being like family, Drake never discussed financial matters in front of her or her sisters. He'd never do something so uncouth. Diana slid her gaze to Minerva, who had a stubborn set to her chin.

Her sister finally turned to Kent. "Nothing, brother, mere speculation upon my part." She leaned forward., Her hand hovered over her bishop before picking up her knight. Diana saw her sister's quick glance at Drake before picking up the piece that she purposefully placed in danger. In essence, Minerva was sacrificing her knight, placing her in the precarious position of potentially losing. Her sister had shared with Diana that she'd hoped Drake would be her knight in shining armor—to save Minerva from her disastrous first Season. Instead, Drake had chosen to spend that Season in gaming halls and ultimately the underbelly hells—that was until their brother Kent rescued him from dun territory. The metaphor of giving up her knight was not lost on Diana, and by the looks of it, it was not lost on Drake either.

Randal shifted and broke the silence. "Lady Minerva, I believe we failed to settle the terms should we find ourselves in a stalemate."

"You are quite right, Lord Chestwick, what do you propose?"

Drake answered, "In the event of a tie, the game is over. No winner. No loser. Nothing more."

Kent laughed. "Whatever is the matter with you Drake, stating the obvious?" He looked over to Randal, "A stalemate is always a possibility. However, none of that matters until the final move is made, and that will not occur unless the game is actually played. Might I suggest that in the event a stalemate were to ensue, a rematch would be scheduled to be played at Malbury Hall?"

Diana swallowed the giggle that threated to escape her. Drake's eyes were wide with shock, and then his brows creased. "Did you or did you not declare that a gentleman could only attempt to play for your hand one time. It is the only reason Mansville has not attempted to trap you into marriage."

The temperature in the room seemed to rise, but it wasn't from the ire rolling off Drake and Minerva. It was due to Randal and his constant gaze at her. While she had pretended to look at each of the others as they spoke, she was very aware of Randal's relaxed posture. She reached for her fan, her favorite accessory to hide behind, but she caught nothing but air at her wrist.

Minerva asked, "You think if Lord Mansville were afforded a second chance, he would best me at a game of chess?"

Drake remained mute, lips drawn tight.

Minerva stood and poked their brother in the chest. "He is *your* friend. Please escort him away, so Lord Chestwick and I can continue without further disturbance."

Dutifully, Kent rose. "Diana, please see to it I'm immediately informed of the outcome as soon as the match concludes."

"It may be hours or mayhap not conclude until the early hours of the morn. Can we simply not discuss this upon our return home tomorrow?"

Randal stiffly stood, his relaxed demeanor gone. "Ladies, please excuse me. I shall return after I've seen Kent and Drake out."

If they were to leave, how was Randal to make Drake jealous? Their plan seemed to be failing rather spectacularly, all because Minerva had positioned the game to end in a stalemate.

Chapter Fourteen

THE JOLT OF panic that ran through his chest at the thought of Diana leaving assaulted his heart in ways Randal never thought possible. He shook his head as he led his guests through the house to the foyer. Minerva had managed to forge an opportunity that would release him from marrying. He should be rejoicing at the clever play, but he wasn't. He was slightly disappointed, which was not at all logical or reasonable.

"Never underestimate a Malbury, but especially not Minerva." Kent donned his coat and gloves and slapped a hand on Drake's shoulder. "Come along, let's pay Cunningham a quick visit. I hear he has restocked his cellar."

Randal waited for the mounted pair to fade into the distance before swiveling on his heels to head back to the library. Years on the battlefield should have prepared him for the onslaught of Malburys. However, his ability to foreshadow his opponent's next move, a skill that had kept him alive all these years, was shattered by these Malbury sisters. He hated feeling lost. It was why he had joined the military. He liked routine, governing rules, and a defined hierarchy that was followed without question. Yet his heart had filled with joy this morning in the breakfast room full of the Malburys' chatter and laughter.

Laughter assaulted his ears as he walked back into the library.

Diana was nestled between Gregory and Minerva as all three were pouring over papers and a stack of books that sat upon the table where the chessboard had sat when he left. He scanned the room for the abandoned game pieces. The match that was to determine Minerva's future, tossed to a side table as if it was of no matter.

Diana was the first to notice his return. She looked directly at him and smiled. The literary poets had got it right—her smile was like a ray of sunshine.

"Randal, come join us. We are having a terrible time with your papa's next clue."

Minerva made room for him but avoided his gaze. In the short time he'd known her, he knew this was odd behavior.

"It would be my pleasure to provide assistance; however, I'd like to speak to Lady Minerva for a moment. In private." He held out his hand and waited for Diana's sister's response.

Minerva ever so lightly placed her hand on his arm. He didn't care for her timid behavior toward him. He may be called a beast, but he would never harm a woman. Randal escorted her over to stand by the bay of windows that streamed in the late afternoon sun.

"I owe you an explanation." Minerva gazed out the window and inhaled deeply before returning her attention back to him. "As I sat down to play, I realized you were right. I had no right to dictate who Diana should marry, nor was it fair of me to demand such a boon from you, whom I've only known for days. However, in my defense, I know all too well the dangers of hiding one's feelings and not acting sooner. The fission of energy when the two of you are in the same room is undeniable. I only wish the best for my sister, and I feel it in my bones—you, my lord, are perfect for her."

"You don't strike me as the type to act upon emotion. Perhaps your feelings for Lord Drake have you behaving in ways you normally would not."

"Mayhap. Although my situation with Drake has no bearing on the fact that Diana is more at ease here with you at Chestwick Hall than at Malbury Manor."

"Or it is simply she is in love with the library."

Minvera laughed. "Books have been Diana's passion since she was in leading strings, but it is your lips that attract her gaze more frequently than she would care to admit. And yours, too. If Kent stayed any longer, he, too, would have noticed the pair of you and your indiscreet glances, and our stay would have been cut short."

"My, you are observant."

"I am, and Kent more so." Minerva sighed and said, "But I must also confess my conscience would not allow me to continue with the ruse. If Drake prefers to remain loyal to Kent in some gentleman code I do not understand, then so be it. My hope is word of our tied game will spur some brave soul, a gentleman other than a fortune hunter, to garner enough courage to sit across the chessboard from me next Season, and I shan't remain a burden to my family."

Burden. To hear Minerva refer to herself as such was heart-wrenching. Women were goddesses to be valued and adored. Randal blinked and squashed the romantic ideal that he once allowed to rule him.

"Then it is your wish we declare our match a stalemate?"

"Aye. And I hope you will not take offense if we do not engage in a rematch at Malbury Manor as Kent suggested." Minerva stared at the windows as she had done earlier. Was she picturing Drake's image in the glass panes?

"If you believe it the best course of action, you have my full support."

Fine wrinkles appeared on her forehead as she gazed up at him. "I appreciate your understanding." Minerva searched his face and abruptly turned her back to him. "Would you mind if I escape to your wonderful gardens? I believe I'd like to spend some time alone."

Randal peered over at Diana and Greg, both pouring over the pile of books and notes in front of them. "I'll give you a head start, but I'm sure your brother will come to check on you shortly."

"My thanks." Without a backward glance, Minerva slipped out through the terrace doors.

Randal waited until she had entered the hedge maze before turning and returning to join Diana and Greg.

Diana glanced up and asked, "Where is Minerva?"

He peered down at the scattered papers and said absently, "She went out to the gardens for a stroll."

"She should not be alone." Worry lines similar to those he had spied on Minerva's forehead moments ago appeared on Diana's beautiful face. Diana shoved her brother's arm. "Gregory, you must go find her."

Glaring at Diana only like a sibling could, Greg rose. His gaze shifted between them both before he shook his head. "Kent won't be happy if he finds out I've left you alone sans chaperone."

"Then you should make haste." Diana grinned and returned her attention back to the stack of papers in front of her.

Greg mumbled, "Bloody, sisters." Dismissed by Diana, he trudged out through the terrace doors.

Never having had one, Randal surmised sisters required extreme amounts of patience. If he were to entertain the idea of marrying Diana, he would gain two sisters along with a wife. The thought should have sent shivers down his spine; instead, a warmth blanketed his heart. With each additional second in her presence, it became more evident to him—Diana Malbury would make an excellent Countess of Chestwick.

MOTIONING TO THE seat her brother had vacated, Diana said, "Come join me." She couldn't wait for Randal to be seated. She blurted the question that had plagued her since Randal had asked to speak to Minerva in private, "What did Minerva share with you? Our plan of making Drake jealous was somewhat successful. Why would she even entertain the idea of a stalemate?"

"I shall answer both your queries once you have answered one of mine." Randal arched an eyebrow. "Do you believe yourself a burden to your family?"

"Aren't all daughters?" Diana asked, falling into old habits of answering a question with a question. It was because Randal was like family. Not an aloof gentleman she didn't wish to spar or converse with.

"Since I have no sisters, I'm unqualified to comment."

Wise reply. She reached for the graphite pencil lodged in her hair and pulled. Her long locks fell about her shoulders. Diana tapped the end of the pencil on the desk, formulating an answer to Randal's question. "The value of a woman is often dictated by the size of her dowry, and thus it is the common belief daughters are naught but a burden." His eyes widened at the sight of her hair unbound. She hastily pulled her locks into another makeshift chignon and jabbed the writing instrument through the center to hold it in place.

"While common, not all men share such foolish ideas." He scanned the documents in front of them and then continued to pick up the volume to his right. Randal nodded as he read the spine. "Which of my papa's clues are you attempting to solve?"

He hadn't answered her questions as he promised. Torn between demanding to know what Minerva had shared with him and continuing her investigation, Diana reached for the worn parchment and read, "Number Three: *Stolen at a glance. Worthless to one, invaluable to two.*"

"Would you care for me to share the answer, or would you prefer I merely provide assistance?"

"Minerva believes it the answer to be love. However, it seems too obvious."

"I would agree with Minerva that love is the solution. Knowing my papa, even after you have solved the eight clues, the answers still may not be exactly as you would expect. I would hazard he would also have foreseen your need for haste."

His soft tone was filled with fond memories as he spoke of his papa. If she was right and Randal did love his papa, why had he stayed away for so long? The man was a puzzle.

"Very well. I shall make note to revisit this clue after we have solved the others."

"We?"

"Since Minerva has escaped, you are the only one left." She lifted the worn parchment in front of her. She could have recited the clue from memory, but she used the paper as a shield, hoping the heat in her cheeks would subside. "Clue number four reads: *Turns. Twirls. Tunes. Three. Two. One.*" She lowered the paper and found Randal grinning. He knew the answer. It was as if his papa had intentionally drafted them for Randal and not for her. "Both Minerva and Greg believe we need to search the library for tomes of music or dance instruction manuals." His grin broadened. Diana said, "Would you agree?"

"I do not." He bent and swooped her into his arms.

She wrapped her arm behind his neck and snuggled closer. She liked the way she fitted perfectly against him. "Where are you taking me?"

"The clue said three turns." His strides were long and purposeful. "It is three turns from the library to the ballroom."

"Did your papa leave you any riddles?"

"Not one in a similar manner to yours." Randal chuckled. "However, there is a pile of correspondence I've not yet managed to work my way through. My papa was not the best estate manager, and our old steward should have been allowed to retire years prior. I've tasked Cartwright with coordinating with the new steward to weed through and sort all the papers."

"I suppose you are looking forward to being rid of us and cease carrying me about, so you can attend to more important matters."

"Cartwright advised me that it would still be another day or two before he would have everything in order for me. And I rather enjoy carting you about. You are a fair amount lighter than the soldiers I'm used to hauling to safety." His grin faded.

"It mustn't have been easy—leaving your men. Knowing they continue to fight while we mull about in safety."

"There are dangers lurking about, just not men with bayonets."

They entered the ballroom, sheets draped over the stacked chairs and tables. Diana had never ventured to this part of the house before. She closed her eyes and let her imagination run free. Glittering candles. The warmth of Randal's hold. She imagined dancing with him, swaying in time to the music.

Randal strode to the center of the room and looked up. A chandelier. Two bars of iron twirled about but in opposite directions. Randal peered down at her. "My papa did not anticipate your injury."

Diana's heart fluttered. "Do you believe he meant for us to dance?"

"Mayhap." He glanced about the room. He tightened his hold on her and approached what looked to be a pianoforte. "Do you know how to play?"

"I am a gently bred lady, am I not?" Diana attempted an offended look.

"Beg pardon, I did not mean to offend."

"Of course I know how to play." Diana let a giggle slip. "I simply do not play well. Isadora's the musician in our family."

"And is Lady Isadora a virtuoso?"

Diana laughed mightily. "Hardly." She leaned forward to remove the dusty cloth and sneezed. If he wasn't holding on to her securely, she would have toppled to the ground. Instead, she found herself in his lap as he took the seat in front of the instrument. He slid her over, and he lifted the lid to reveal the ivory keys.

"Do you play?"

"I am a gentleman, am I not?" He teased.

Discovering this more refined side of Randal was both pleasing and perturbing.

He interlocked his long fingers and stretched them. Fingers that had been wound around her waist were now poised over the keys.

"We are missing the sheet music."

He began to play, and his eyelids closed, covering his dual-toned eyes. "Do you recognize the tune?"

She closed her eyes and tried to concentrate on the melody, not the feel of his arm next to hers. "Nay."

"Listen closely."

She did, and the vibration of the notes flowed through her. She opened her eyes to peek at Randal. It struck her he was classically handsome in the family portraits, but in real life, his features were scarred, but it gave him a wealth of character, and she wanted to learn about all his adventures and experiences. The melody became familiar, yet she couldn't recall its name.

He opened his eyes. "Can you guess?"

"I believe I have heard this when I was younger."

"You may have."

"Is it the piece purported to be of Orpheus and Eurydice?"

"Aye. It was written to convey Orpheus's desire to see Eurydice once again, to resurrect her from the underworld."

"I can feel the longing…the need…the deep pull…when you play the song." She looked at him quizzically. "Are you the composer?"

Randal laughed. "I am old but not that old. I believe neither of us was born when this was first performed." Eyes closed, his fingers glided over the ivory keys. Randal's arm brushed against her, and it was as if the music flowed through him and straight to her heart.

"What does the song mean to you?"

"After my mama died, my papa played this late at night when he believed my brother and I were fast asleep." He abruptly stopped playing. "My mama was his world, and when she departed, she took the best part of him with her." His spine stiffened, and a chill ran down Diana's back. She didn't believe in ghosts, but there was a distinct shift in the air about them. Randal shifted closer and bent to pick her up once more.

Seeking out his warmth, she wrapped her arm securely around his neck and settled into his arms. "I'm not certain we have found the answer to this clue."

"I would agree." He carried her to the opposite corner and stopped. "The solution must be here."

She peered over his shoulder, and when she leaned back, her cheek grazed his. Without thought, she wrapped both arms about his neck and brought his head down to hers. She searched his eyes and pressed her lips to his. He tightened his hold and widened his stance.

Tilting her head to one side, Diana asked, "Does kissing always leave one breathless?"

"No."

"Perhaps I was doing it wrong. Should we try again?"

"No."

"Did you not enjoy our first kiss?"

"I immensely enjoyed our first and our second." Warmth radiated from his body as he held her tight, his gaze smoldering with an emotion she could not ignore—why would she want to?

He was counting the kiss in the field, which had been rather shocking and exciting, but this...this kiss is the one she would always consider their first. She hoped for more.

Diana smiled. "We should return to the library."

"As you wish."

Chapter Fifteen

Randal wanted to hold on to Diana as long as possible. The interlude in the ballroom left him nearly panting once more—it was merely a kiss. Yet it had been far more intimate, even more so than any of his past sexual encounters with women. His feet took them back to the library, but his mind wandered—images of Diana laying across his bed in his chambers floated before him. He ran his tongue over the edge of his teeth at the thought, but she was an innocent. He straightened and readjusted his arms, so there was no chance of his forearm brushing against her bosom.

"Am I getting too heavy?"

"Not in the least."

She placed a hand on his cheek. "Are you certain? My ankle feels much better. I do believe I could walk."

He paused and stood a few feet away from the library door. "I like having you close."

"I like being in your arms." She ran her hand down the side of his neck and laid it flat against his chest, where his heart continued to thump erratically. "If Minerva and Greg have returned from their walk outdoors, will you remain to assist me with the remaining clues?"

"Would you like for me to stay and assist?"

"I would."

The woman was dangerous. She fed his yearning to be needed. If he spent more time with Diana, would he let be able to her go? Would she want to stay? Needing answers, Randal asked, "What if we completed all four remaining clues this afternoon? You will no longer have a reason to return."

Tapping her forefinger against her flushed cheek, Diana replied, "Hmm... I can think of a reason."

"Care to share it with me?"

"You." She shifted and placed a chaste kiss on his jawline and settled back into his arms as if there was no more to be said.

A gale of laughter wafted down the hall, prompting Randal to move again. "We should join your family."

"Wait." She lifted her palm to her cheek. "Are they still red?"

He glanced down. Her cheeks were a pretty pink but no longer rose red. "No. Are mine?"

She tilted her head. No meek fluttering of her eyelashes, simply an honest stare. She giggled. "A little."

What? Surely his suntanned face hid his blush.

She wrapped her arm around the back of his neck once more and ran a finger down the side of his neck.

Randal chuckled. "Minx, it is all your fault."

"I'm proud to be the cause."

He shook his head and headed for the library, confused by Diana's innate ability to make him smile and evoke within him a sense of happiness he had long forgotten but was glad to know he was still capable of experiencing.

Preoccupied with thoughts, he waited for Diana to open the door. He took three steps into the room and froze. Unprepared for the sight of Minerva and Greg engaged in a battle of pillows. Although he and his brother had only been two years apart in age, they never played together as children, and as adults rarely shared the same interests, with the exception that they both joined His Majesty's army to fight the Frogs. The one thing they shared, and it had led to his brother's death.

Diana leaned her forehead against his shoulder. "I apologize for their childish behavior."

"It is rather refreshing to see Minerva with her guard down."

"She really is perfect."

"Mayhap for Drake, but not for me."

"What makes you certain?"

"They are opposites. Drake portrays himself as relaxed and uncaring, while I suspect he really is the serious sort, and Minerva is perceived to be controlled and somber, except those who know her well know she is playful and fun."

Diana frowned, "I don't believe our ruse to make Drake jealous worked."

"Your sister shared with me her rational for abandoning the plan, and Minerva is right—if Drake can't figure it out on his own, he doesn't deserve her."

"I can't believe he could be that dimwitted not to realize what is right before him."

"Some men are not as smart as I."

"Oh, is that so?" She smiled. "You shall have to prove to me how smart you really are…by assisting me with your papa's blasted clues."

He crept closer to the desk, attempting to remain unnoticed but failed.

Minerva yelped, "Oh, you have returned." She rushed to Diana's side and bent low to whisper, "I apologize it didn't occur to me you might need to visit the privy."

Diana groaned. "We were working on solving the next clue."

"Oh." Minerva twisted to return the pillow to the settee. "What did you find?"

"The clue led us to the ballroom."

"Ballroom!" Minerva picked up the parchment with the clues that remained on the desk. "Good gracious, we never would have deciphered that without Chestwick's assistance. Well, what did you find?" Randal's mind reeled from the numerous discoveries he had made in the ballroom, but none had to do with his papa's riddles.

Diana extracted the wooden graphite from her hair and spoke as she wrote, "Ballroom. Dancing. Sheet music. Pianoforte. Melody." She followed the words with a series of question marks.

Minerva said, "Add *songs* to the list."

Diana peered up at her sister, then shook her head and did as her sister had bid—adding the word *songs*. Watching the siblings work in harmony was enlightening and invoked a strange hunger within Randal—did he want to become a member of this unruly lot? Unstructured days. No defined purpose. The life of an idle gentleman—his mind screamed at him to attend to his affairs and return to his men, but his heart tugged at the thought of leaving Diana.

Minerva squinted at the paper and read aloud. "Clue number five: I have eighty-five keys. None unlock any doors, but they are fundamental to me."

Greg stretched his long arms out and placed his hands behind his head. "I'm aghast you spent your summers muddling over riddles such as these."

Diana stiffened at her brother's statement. "Is that so? I presume you believe you have the answer."

"I do not." Greg smiled. "Mayhap my mind works best dealing with facts. Not obscure references."

Diana looked up, and her lips moved, counting in silence. Randal was so preoccupied fantasizing over those lips, he was slow to react when a pillow went flying past him, hitting Gregory in the head.

Minerva said, "My dear brother, if you are not going to be of assistance, I suggest you take yourself elsewhere."

"And miss all the fun." Greg hugged the pillow to his chest and closed his eyes.

Minerva returned her attention to the paper. "Eighty-five."

Diana glanced at him and mouthed, "Do you know?"

Randal wanted to say yes, but with his mind on pillows, he was toying with the idea of whisking her way to his chambers, not on his papa's riddles. He cleared his throat and asked, "Minerva, could you please repeat the clue once more?"

Minerva handed him the paper and began to pace, her whole attention was on solving the riddle, which is what he should be focused upon, too.

He read over the clue twice before saying. "I believe this riddle was to be solved in conjunction with the prior one."

Diana asked, "How so?"

The sweet lilt of her voice captured his full regard. "Clue number four led us to the ballroom. But once in the ballroom, where did it lead us?"

Diana's eyes went wide with recognition. "How clever of you, my lord—the pianoforte!"

The compliment flipped his heart with joy Yet alarm bells rang in his head. He needed space before he acted rashly. However, his bottom remained firmly seated in the chair next to the woman whom he was rapidly falling in love with.

Chapter Sixteen

Silenced by the frosty look that clouded Randal's eyes, Diana busied herself with rearranging papers. All Season long, gentleman after gentleman had disappointed Diana. Most referred to her love of word puzzles as plain ridiculousness; others simply gave her the cut direct and left her alone, never to approach again. Despite his original objections, Randal had assisted her with every clue. It was clear that the man was clever, yet intelligence alone wouldn't have allowed him to solve the clues—only a fellow lover of prose knew better than to simply take a word at face value.

Her heart stopped. Her gaze affixed to Randal's relaxed features. Randal Wilson—Earl of Chestwick—the brilliant war strategist—the Beast of Chestwick—was the man she had been searching for.

The legs of Randal's chair scraped against the floor, breaking her train of thought. With a curt nod, he left her to meander across the room to sit in the chair opposite to Greg. Her body swayed slightly forward, the intangible pull that had her wanting to be close to the man was growing in intensity. Her brother, who rarely found much to say to strangers, was openly conversing with Randal as if he was one of the family. Her siblings openly accepted Randal, unlike the few brave gentleman callers who had arrived at the Malbury townhouse with flowers this past Season.

With no one else close, Diana sat back and seized the moment to admire Randal's profile. It was no wonder that Randal had been a successful army captain. His strength came from both his quick mind and his muscular form. She rubbed her palms together, recalling the feel of his hard broad chest. Randal was unlike any scholar she had ever been acquainted with.

Minerva stepped in front, blocking her view of the man. "Stop staring at him like he's a treat you wish to devour."

"I was doing no such thing."

"Oh yes, you were." Minerva placed her hands on her hips. "You claimed you wanted to find old Lord Chestwick's prized literary piece before we depart in the morn...did you not?"

Randal had been right. If they solved the mystery this afternoon, what plausible reason would she have to return? None that Minerva would believe. The only excuse Diana would have—wanting to spend time with Randal. So, she didn't want the riddle to be solved.

"Diana." Minerva's gaze bore down upon her. "We still have two or three more riddles to solve. If we concentrate, I'm certain we shall be successful. It is still the goal to obtain the treasure and leave Chestwick alone—correct?" With a slight shake of her head, Minerva said, "No need to reply—clearly it is no longer our primary objective." She looked about and then added, "Perhaps, I should suggest Chestwick and I finish the game we started. If I take an extra moment or two to ponder over my moves, I could draw out the game until suppertime, and then we can officially declare the game a tie."

Diana insanely wanted Randal's attention for herself, not to watch him sit across from Minerva.

As if Minerva could read her mind, her sister added, "I promise not to prolong the game longer than necessary and, leaving the riddle unsolved, you shall have a logical reason to return at a later time—chaperoned, of course."

Diana smiled. She wished she could have somehow made Minerva's wishes come to fruition as her sister did for her. "Will you assist me to stand? I'd like to watch the game."

"Are you certain your ankle is healed enough to bear weight?"

"Aye, I made it to the water closet unassisted earlier. However, it is a tad sore now."

"Diana Malbury! Here I believed you were still in pain since you have let Chestwick carry you about like a babe, when in fact you have simply been enjoying his beastly attention."

"He's not a beast."

"He's hardly what one would call charming. He rarely smiles. His lips only curve a twinge in your direction. He barely speaks unless to bark orders…"

Minerva shifted closer, and Diana rested a hand on her sister's arm. "That is because everyone else hardly ever pauses to take a breath."

"True." Minerva smiled and whispered, "Shall we wager how many paces before Chestwick swoops you up? Say half a month's allowance?"

Diana had lost on the last two wagers she'd made during the Season with Minerva. The reasons for her sister's wish to amass a large sum alluded her. Minerva was not one to run away from the family. She loved and cared for them too much to cause such angst and worry. "Very well, five."

"Ha. I'll wager is it no more than three."

Minerva shifted, allowing her to take a step forward, placing weight on her good leg.

To Diana's delight, she was in Chestwick's arms before the heel of her injured foot even touched the floor.

He frowned down at her. "What do you think you are doing?"

She wound her arm behind his neck, "I was making my way toward the chessboard."

"Whatever for?"

"Kent will be expecting an update, and Minerva believes it shan't take long to complete the game." She stroked the back of his neck. She delighted in the feel of the strong, corded muscles flexing beneath her fingertips.

"I presumed it a foregone conclusion, and thus there was no need to continue playing."

"Malburys never leave anything unfinished."

Randal chuckled. "Duly noted." He bent to settle her upon the chair next to the chessboard.

The temptation to graze her lips over his as he slowly retreated was great but with both Minerva and Greg watching, she dared not declare her feelings just quite yet. She would trust Minerva not to say a word, but Greg would be honor-bound to demand Randal offer for her hand. While her heart screamed yes, her mind was cautiously waiting to find the treasure first.

She gradually removed her arm and peered up at him. "Minerva likes a challenge."

Randal gave her a wink and said, "I do, too."

He moved to take his seat opposite Minerva, who was patiently waiting with her hands in her lap, staring at the pieces as if she was attempting to move them with her mind.

"I believe it is your turn, Lady Minerva," Randal said.

"It is indeed, Lord Chestwick. I simply wish to refresh my memory as to the probabilities."

"Please, take your time." He sat back and stared at Diana.

His gaze never wavered from her lips. He shifted slightly in his chair, breaking her sister's concentration once again.

"Lord Chestwick, is there something wrong?"

His skin reddened, highlighting the scar that appeared even more white against his flushed cheeks. "I don't believe so. Is it my turn?"

Minerva's narrowed gaze flickered between them and then landed upon her. "Stop distracting the man. You don't want him to lose, do you?"

"Is that even a possibility?"

"Of course it is. Playing to tie is complicated."

Diana bowed her head. "My apologies. I shan't make this more difficult than need be."

"I shouldn't have snapped at you." Minerva placed a hand on her arm and then added, "You, Lord Chestwick, need to pay attention to the game."

"My apologies." Randal said the words but hardly looked apologetic.

She gave her head a little shake as his fingers hovered over his rook and smiled as he picked up his knight.

Minerva turned to face Diana. "He needs no assistance from you."

"Exactly how many ways are there to tie a game?"

Minerva focused on the chess pieces before she absently answered, "I know of three."

Diana sighed in relief and sat back to wait for the game to end. If Minerva had three ways in which to achieve a stalemate, she had little to worry about.

Chapter Seventeen

Randal studied the board but kept Diana within his peripheral vision. Minerva claimed there to be three possible ways to tie the game. Three. He was only familiar with two. The first being where each player was limited to repeating the same maneuvers over and over without placing the other in check, which he unfortunately had often encountered on the battlefield during more than one skirmish. The second being where no legal moves were available, also a situation he had encountered on the battlefield.

Leaning back in his chair, Randal faced his opponent. "In the interest of time, mayhap you could enlighten me as to the three situations in which a stalemate may be declared."

"The first—no legal moves. The second—insufficient pieces. The third is by agreement due to repetition."

The Malburys might think him a dullard, but he asked anyway, "Pray elaborate upon the second."

"A stalemate will ensue if you do not have the pieces necessary to both check the king and, at the same time, make sure he has no way to escape."

"Ah, so not so much a matter of how many pieces but which pieces remain." Taking an extra moment to indulge in viewing Diana's lips that were curved into a smile, Randal pretended to mull over the possibilities. Reluctantly, he returned his attention back to his opponent, whose gaze flickered between him and Diana.

Randal said, "Do I understand correctly that if I retain a king and a rook, it is still possible for me to win, but if I'm left with only a king and a knight or mayhap a bishop, a tie will be the end result."

Both Diana and Minerva answered in unison. "Exactly."

He looked down at the chessboard and reassessed his pieces and their positions. Diana's breath hitched ever so slightly. No one else seemed to have noticed her reaction except for him, which was not surprising since he was ultra-conscious of her every move. It was still possible for him to win the game.

Minerva made her move, and Diana's shoulders sagged. Did the woman have so little faith in him? Randal's mind wandered from the game. What was he doing? He never placed one person's wishes above the greater good for all involved. Caring for and loving another was extremely dangerous, and he had purposefully avoided forming attachments for years—a task made easier by remaining upon the war-torn Continent. Why should he alter his stance now? Again, his gaze was drawn to Diana.

Refocusing on the game before him, Randal noted he could easily place his rook in jeopardy, but that wouldn't be playing to win, and he suspected both Diana and Minerva would never respect him if he purposefully played to tie. Calling upon experiences learned on the battlefield, Randal knew taking time to build a solid defense before launching an aggressive attack was a winning strategy. Should he win, it would mean he'd have to marry Minerva. His stomach tightened into knots.

"Lord Chestwick, it is your move," Minerva prompted.

He glanced over at Diana, who was still avoiding his gaze. He didn't need her help, but it was nice for a moment to believe he was partnering with another, that he wasn't all alone in this battle.

He spread his legs and rested his forearms over his knees. Closer and lower to the board, it afforded him a different angle and perspective. However, from the corner of his eye, it also placed Diana's décolleté in plain sight, which was distracting. *Very distracting.*

He considered his possible moves carefully, attempting to play each scenario out two moves ahead. He frowned up at Minerva. He didn't know the woman as well as he knew the French military tactics employed on the battlefield. If he could maneuver hundreds of men into position, surely, he could figure out how to maneuver chess pieces into formation.

Diana shifted—the edge of her gown lowering ever so slightly. If he were to get her alone one more time before her departure, he needed the game to be completed quickly. He straightened and moved his pawn into a defensive position.

Diana beamed a smile in his direction. "Well played."

A burst of pride rushed through his veins. To be the cause for Diana's sweet smile motivated Randal to focus on the board once again.

Minerva sat back and crossed her arms.

Greg chuckled and said, "It would appear Chestwick, you have surprised both my dear sisters." He pulled up a chair, clearly with the intention of watching the match play out. "Most opponents Minerva has played have been the aggressor. A defensive play was both unexpected and genius. I'm looking forward to seeing what Minerva's next move shall be."

"A play-by-play commentary is not required." Minerva scowled at her brother. "I shall simply reconsider my strategy."

A ruckus of male voices wafted through the walls. He hadn't expected Kent and Drake to return. He stood to send the men away once again.

The door swung open, and his butler announced, "Lord Mansville and Lord Tierney."

Moving towards the strangers, Randal's knuckles cracked as his hand balled into a fist. Lord Mansville was the gentleman Kent spoke of that had caused Minerva such distress. He stood before his unwanted and uninvited guests.

"Lord Chestwick, it is an honor to make your acquaintance." Lord Mansville glanced and nodded to Gregory, who was now standing next to Randal. "Mr. Malbury." Slapping the back of his hand on his companion's chest, Lord Mansville said, "Look, Tierney. The lovely Malbury sisters are present."

Lord Tierney appeared chagrined by Lord Mansville's rude behaviour. "Lord Chestwick, our apologies for intruding."

Gregory shifted slightly to block the scoundrel's view of his sisters. "Mansville—what the devil are you doing here?"

"We were riding back to London, and my horse fell lame."

Lord Mansville took a step forward, and Randal shifted to his left to block the rude guest from getting any closer to the women. "That is easily remedied. I have a full stable with a fine array of horses at the ready. Let us adjourn to the stables."

Stepping around both Greg and Randal, Lord Mansville made his way over to the ladies. "Oh, but I see that Lady Minerva is engaged in playing a game of chess." Lord Mansville loomed over Minerva. "Who is your opponent, Lady Minerva?"

Minerva stood and glared at the man. Diana's sister bravely faced her nemesis with her shoulders rolled back as if she was ready to argue with Lord Mansville. However, Randal noted Minerva was taking shallow breaths.

Mansville stepped closer, crowding Minerva. The gentleman was proving to be as vile as Drake made him out to be. Randal glanced at the women once more. The fear in both Diana and Minerva's eyes sent sparks of anger through Randal. Coming to stand behind Diana, who had lowered her injured leg, Randal barked, "I am."

Chapter Eighteen

Randal's voice boomed through the room and rattled Diana's bones. Her palms began to sweat. It was sweet that Randal was coming to Minerva's defense, but there was no chance that Lord Mansville would leave before the game concluded, and Lord Tierney would no doubt ensure that the outcome of this match would be spread through the *ton* swiftly. The stakes of the game had tripled, and Diana found herself conflicted as what outcome would be best for her sister.

Minerva would do anything for her. Was Diana willing to forgo what she believed to be a blossoming love for Randal? Randal was, first and foremost, a soldier. The man fought for causes he believed in. He was a defender. The terrifying glare Randal was giving Lord Mansville would have most gentlemen excusing themselves and running, except Lord Mansville, the wastrel, was obsessed with studying the chess-board and Minerva.

Lord Mansville settled into the seat Greg had previously occupied, he crossed his legs and then his arms, radiating an air of ease that Diana knew was false. The vile man tore his gaze from Minerva to address Randal. "Lord Chestwick, what fortuitous timing. I enjoy witnessing all of Lady Minerva's chess matches."

The skin on the back of Diana's neck prickled as the lecherous Lord Tierney approached. "You will have excuse Mansville's egregious behavior, he loses all of his senses in the presence of Lady Minerva. He is obsessed with the woman. When he's not in the same room as she, he's actually quite rational." The lack of etiquette displayed by both men had Diana clenching her hands at her side. Lord Tierney was a *liar.* Mansville was never rational.

Diana silently prayed Randal would not believe the falsehoods Lord Tierney was spouting. She scooted forward to the edge of her chair and jumped as Randal rested a hand upon her shoulder.

He bent to speak into her ear. "I won't let any harm come to you or Minerva. Trust me."

Her shoulders relaxed. Leaning back so she could face him, Diana smiled and said, "I do trust you."

Randal rounded the settee and strode to stand next to the chessboard. "Lord Tierney, I believe a seat over next to Lord Mansville shall afford you the best view of the game." His voice was hard and restrained, much like it had been upon finding her dangling from a ladder the first day of her visit.

Randal signaled for a footman and a sour-faced Paul came forward with a chair and situated it to the left of Mansville but a full arm's length away from Randal.

A knot formed in Diana's stomach as Randal took his seat opposite Minerva. She glanced at her sister, whose complexion was pale. Mansville had terrorized Minerva at every event they attended. He made it a point to ask Minerva for the first dance of every ball and thus forced her to remain on the outskirts of the dance floor once she declined his request. The man even managed to wedge himself or one of his cronies next to Minerva at every opportunity when their brother Kent or Greg were absent and made lewd remarks that were intended to unravel Minerva's cool exterior.

At first her sister ignored the vile men, but by the end of the Season, Minerva's defenses were in tatters. Diana and Isadora never left Minerva's side, which heightened their mama's ire—for none of them danced, promenaded, or conversed with any of the eligible gentlemen that were thrust upon them.

Diana searched the room for Greg, but he was nowhere in sight. How long had he been gone? They needed Kent. Mansville was a skilled chess player; he would immediately call foul if either Minerva or Randal threw the game. If he accused Minerva of such, Minerva needed Kent to be present.

She clasped her hands tight in her lap and glanced at her sister. Diana silently mouthed, "Stay calm. All will be well."

Minerva woodenly nodded. "My apologies, please remind me, whose turn is it?"

Lord Mansville sneered, "Chestwick, don't be deceived by Lady Minerva's sweet tone and innocent looks. I'm certain she is quite aware of exactly who should recommence play and where each piece remains and has a stratagem to lure you into playing into her trap."

Lord Mansville, for once, was telling the truth—Minerva would know exactly what and how many moves were necessary to win, but Minerva wasn't playing to win. Mayhap her sister should be. Diana glanced at Mansville and Tierney. They may be members of the peerage and referred to as gentleman, but their souls were dark and evil.

She shifted her gaze over to Randal. Here was a good, honorable man who could provide a life for her sister. She crossed her arms and pressed against her stomach, which was knotted and aching. What a terrible sister she was. It was selfish to want Randal for herself. To want the man that could save her sister from torment and pain. Every inch of Diana's body ached to be back in the security of Randal's arms. She bowed her head and blinked back the tears that were forming. Randal would make Minerva a wonderful husband. Her sister could be happy here at Chestwick Hall, and Minerva would never have to endure another horrid Season.

She had failed to provoke Drake to take action all Season and, even with Randal's assistance, she had failed to assist Minerva in gaining the man who had captured and then disabused her sister's heart. Drake was a fool—he had done nothing to prevent the current match between Randal and Minerva from occurring.

Eyes blurry with moisture, Diana stared at the two unwanted guests once more. Lord Mansville was deep in thought, studying the board, while Lord Tierney was blatantly gazing at Minerva's décolleté. Where did Diana's loyalties lie? To her sister or to a man who she only recently met.

Chapter Nineteen

THE WOOD CARVINGS were a blur. Randal's brain screamed at him to win the game and protect Minerva from the ghastly men seated to his right. His heart yearned for the woman's sister and ached with the remaining shreds of faith he possessed. Faith that all would work out in the favor of love. The intangible pull that had kept him close to Diana remained, but the slight turn of her body had Randal viewing her back instead of her alluring face. Unable to decipher his own conflicted thoughts, he was hoping Diana would give him a signal as to her own thoughts.

"It appears you have found yourself a worthy opponent Lady Minerva." Lord Mansville's statement drew Randal's attention back to the despicable man.

For years on the battlefield, he'd been surrounded by men of all characters. Randal found those with Mansville's temperament tended to be emotionally immature and thus sought out the weak to pray upon and only gained pleasure from the suffering of others. He detested men like Mansville.

Minerva's cheeks gained a little more color. "Aye, Lord Chestwick does indeed live up to his reputation as a brave and brilliant war strategist."

He expected her to reach out to make her next move, but she seemed hesitant. He wanted to box Mansville's ears for causing such anxiety and discomfort. However, gentlemen didn't resort to fistfights to settle matters as they did in the army, especially in the presence of women.

Randal's lungs were devoid of air at the thought of his men and the war. He had left them to fend for themselves and face the bloodshed without him. He promised himself he would return to fight by their side within a year. A year should have been sufficient time for him to assume his title of earl, fortify the estate that had languished from generations of scholarly management, marry, and sire an heir. However, he had not anticipated the complication of finding himself entangled with Diana Malbury. It seemed as if his entire world had shifted the moment the woman had raked her hands over his body.

His gaze was drawn to Diana once more, but it was as if time had stopped while he ruminated over the past and present. No one had moved. Diana remained facing away from him, while Minerva perched on the edge of her seat appeared to be either preparing to gather her courage and bolt from the room or make a bold move in the game. Diana's spine stiffened as Minerva's slight hand hovered over her king.

Randal desperately wished he could will Diana to look at him. He wanted to reach for her to comfort her. What was he thinking? He glanced at Mansville and Tierney, who hovered close like vultures ready to pick the flesh off the bones of its prey. Becoming involved with the Malbury family would be like signing up for war of a different nature. A battle waged in drawing rooms, at balls, and soirees. His stratagems that had proved successful against the Frogs hardly seemed appropriate against foes like Mansville and Tierney. The Malburys were an intelligent lot. They were in no need of his assistance.

Minerva raised her hand to pick up her knight and completed her turn. Was she sending Randal a message by selecting the knight rather than the king?

Manville shot to his feet. "Lady Minerva! You disappoint me—you are not playing to win."

Randal stood to face the man that was a peer but was no better than a Frog in Randal's opinion. He wanted to grab Mansville and his crony by the scruff and tell them to get the bloody hell off his estate and to never dare step foot upon his land again. Societal rules that he'd not had to abide by for years but had been drummed into his head as a young man prevented him from doing so.

Before Randal could act, the hard wooden library door hit the wall as Kent, followed by Greg, burst through into the room and marched to stand next to Minerva. "Mansville, are you accusing my sister of dishonorable play?" Kent's deep voice echoed off the walls.

Mansville swiveled to face Kent. "L-lord Kent. Were you aware of this façade?"

Kent's dark scowl was rather impressive. A look that Randal had not thought him capable of. Randal took a step closer to Diana, intending to pick her up and move her to a safer location in the room should a brawl erupt.

Slightly bent at the waist, Diana stalled his movements with a fierce whisper. "Do not even consider carrying me about in front of those jackals." She placed her hand in Minerva's, who had joined them.

Minerva said, "I'll assist her while you lend support to our brother."

Diana rose and leaned on her sister's arm for support. A twinge of pain or jealousy that Diana chose to seek out her sister's aid and not his hit him squarely in the chest.

Burying the unwanted emotion, Randal walked around to deal with his unwanted guests. "Gentleman, let's adjourn to my private study to discuss the matter." He waved a hand toward the door, and, surprisingly, both Mansville and Tierney moved to leave without objection. Kent and Greg followed suit. As Randal made his way, he looked over his shoulder to see Diana consoling Minerva, whose head was cradled in her hands. He wasn't certain what was to come of his next discussion, but he knew it would determine his future.

Chapter Twenty

ROLES REVERSED, DIANA rubbed large circles over her older sister's back. It was refreshing to be able to be the one to console Minerva. Her sister, who never wavered, who was the family pilar, who was always the first to comfort Diana, was currently a nervous wreck. Diana and her sisters had believed the blasted challenge to win a chess game for Minerva's hand a stroke of brilliance three years ago, but now it was proving to be the worst scheme they had ever engaged in.

Minerva rolled her head from side to side, "Kent will let his anger get the best of him and no doubt challenge Mansville to a duel. He'll die, and it will be my fault. All because I wanted to avoid marriage. Why did I ever concoct such an idiotic idea?"

Diana tried to piece together words that would help alleviate Minerva's fears. Wasn't she the sister known for her flair for words and books? Surely, she should be able to find the right words. Except her mind was blank, and her stomach was in knots.

Minerva peeked from behind her fingers. "Lord Mansville makes me nervous."

"He's a scoundrel and a bully." Diana pried Minerva's hand away from her face. "He can't challenge you again. You are safe."

Her sister shook her head. "I won't be safe unless…"

Diana interrupted. "Unless you marry! You should lose and marry

Randal. He's smart, honorable, and he'd make you a fine husband."

Minerva straightened and took Diana's hand in hers. "No. Lord Chestwick would tolerate me like papa endures mama. There is no escape from marriage to the wrong man. However, I am of the belief Lord Chestwick would make *you* a very fine husband."

"Why would you say something so absurd?"

"Mayhap it is due to the fact that the man shares your love of literature..." Minerva paused and ran her thumb over Diana's brow. "And like you, he has the propensity to seek out adventure. I don't know the man well enough to deduce his exact reasoning for spending all those years on the battlefield, but it is clear to me he is perfect for you."

Diana let go of her sister's hand. "Have you gone mad? He's known for being a beast..." But she could not hide her tiny smile.

"And that is precisely why you are drawn to him. Lord Chestwick is built like a warrior unlike any other gentleman of our acquaintance. It is no surprise to me that you find the man attractive. I'd wager all my pin money that he makes you feel wanted, secure, protected, all the things mama has been denied all these years."

Diana blinked twice. "Mansville's appearance has muddled your mind. You are mistaken."

Minerva rarely gambled. For her sister to place her entire savings at risk meant there was no changing her mind. "I suspect Lord Chestwick bears deep internal scars that were inflicted well before he ever stepped foot upon the Continent. Wounds that are in need of healing. My hypothesis is that Lord Chestwick's papa had hoped your shared love of riddles would bring the two of you together."

"Are you suggesting Randal's papa tricked me?"

Minerva's gaze flickered toward the door that the men had exited through. "Tricked? Or was it merely an old man's attempt at matchmaking? I'm sure it was carried out with no malice."

"How blind I have been!" Diana's hands balled into fists.

"I don't understand." Minerva frowned. "I thought you were beginning to form an attachment to Chestwick?"

Her sister, as usual, was correct. She had let her fascination with Randal's image influence her interactions with the man in the flesh. To fancy a man she had only met a few days ago was insanity, and to believe she was in love was preposterous. She was the one who had lost her wits, not Minerva. Diana stared at her sister. She wanted to be like Minerva, bold and daring, to be the master of her own destiny. Randal's papa must have written to Randal and disclosed all her preferences, which would be why he had been able to disarm her defenses. Or had Randall's papa secretly brought them together?

Pushing her confused thoughts from her mind, Diana looked her sister squarely in the eyes. "Mansville will continue to be a nuisance until you marry."

"I concur." Minerva stared at the tips of her toes that peeked out from beneath her skirts. "I need just a little more time."

"You have a plan to bring Drake to heel?"

Minerva mumbled, "I wish for a husband who wants to marry me and not enter wedlock out of trickery."

Diana stared at her sister. "I want the same." Her shoulders relaxed.

Thundering male voices wafted into the room. In addition to the deep baritones of Chestwick and her brothers, Diana recognized the voices of Drake and Cunningham. It was no surprise to Diana that the pair had also arrived. The servants were notorious for gossiping amongst the four households.

One by one, the scowling gentlemen waltzed past the butler, who held the door open for them. None of them even glanced at Minerva or Diana. Each marched across the room with determination toward the awaiting chessboard.

Randal was the first to utter a sound. *Randal.* His name bobbled about in her head. She should really refer to him as Lord Chestwick or by his title, at the very least, and not his given name, even if he had given her permission. It was too intimate, and if Minera lost the game, Randal would be her brother-in-law. With a mental nod, Diana resolved to refer to the man as Chestwick.

Chin pointed in the direction of the chessboard, Chestwick said, "Study the pieces again Mansville. As I explained, it is not only possible but most likely that Lady Minerva's stratagem is to lure me into believing I'm winning when in fact she is establishing her pieces to win in the least number of moves given my last counter move."

Chestwick's severe, serious gaze never wavered from the board. It was obvious that he was not at all happy at the turn of events. He was probably cursing her for embroiling him in the convoluted mess her family had created for themselves.

Mansville sat in the chair Minerva had occupied and then got up to sit in Randal's chair. *Blast.* Chestwick, not Randal. How was she to distance her heart if she couldn't even manage to do so mentally? After a long moment, Manville glanced at Minerva and then back to Randal.

"Lord Chestwick, for once, the gossip mill is correct. You are a brilliant strategist." He stood and moved to face her brother. "Lord Kent, I offer my apologies for rudely interrupting the game. I shall agree to remain an impartial witness going forward."

"Your apology is misdirected." Kent's response was issued in a clipped tone that he rarely used. Instead of issuing another apology to Minerva, Mansville slid back into the chair he'd vacated earlier and idly crossed his legs.

Why didn't one of the men simply throw the jackal out?

Diana stared at Randal, waiting for him to dispense with the devil. Instead, he approached them, and winged his arm for Minerva.

Chestwick escorted her sister the short distance back to the game. The stone set of his face and the determined set of his shoulders led Diana to believe whatever the discussion that had transpired in the study—Chestwick was ready to be rid of her and her family.

Chapter Twenty-One

After two hours of sitting in the same chair, Randal rubbed his head in frustration. He wasn't accustomed to remaining idle for such long periods. Wishing the chess game to be done, Randal glanced at the crestfallen woman seated across from him. He waited for Lady Minerva to evaluate the few remaining pieces on the board and to determine their fate. Mansville's mean-spirited remarks and Tierney's lecherous looks had Minerva constantly glancing nervously at her brother Kent, whose watchful gaze did nothing to bolster his sister's confidence.

Minerva was no longer the self-confident, spirited lady he'd come to know. Why men felt the need to belittle or undermine the strength of a woman, he would never come to understand. It wasn't pity that caused a horrid caustic feeling to settle in his lower stomach. It was his empathetic tendencies. He'd gone off to battle, hoping the propensity to feel what others felt would dissipate in the face of mass death and destruction. He had been wrong. The war had only heightened the predisposition, which reinforced his need to remain and assist in winning the war, so his men could return home to their families. The bitter taste of leaving a task incomplete remained at the back of Randal's throat.

For the hundredth time, Drake tugged at his cravat, drawing both Randal and Minerva's attention. Minerva scowled at Drake while

Randal took advantage of the opportunity to gaze upon the woman who he couldn't banish from his thoughts. He should be concentrating entirely on the game before him, given the stakes, but the magnetic pull had him glancing at Diana every chance he could, only to be disappointed to find her studying the game board and not him. It was incredulous to want a woman so completely after spending a few days in her company.

Minerva reached for her queen, and Drake coughed, drawing everyone's attention this time.

"I hope you aren't falling ill Lord Drake," Minerva said as she picked up the piece and twirled it between her fingers. "Summer colds are the worst." The chill in Minerva's voice almost had Randal rubbing his arms.

"Ahh, and the Ice Queen finally reemerges." Mansville's quip received glares from all, especially from Drake.

Kent stood and barked, "Refer to my sister as the Ice Queen once more, and I'll see you at dawn."

Minerva turned to her brother. "Benedict, no. Please don't." She quickly placed her queen next to Randal's pawn.

Randal did a double take at the board and the pieces. What was Minerva doing? Under the watchful gaze of Mansville, he had carefully planned each move, allowing Minerva at least two viable options to either win or cease the game in a tie. However, it was not easy to disguise every move, ensuring Mansville would have no cause to call into question his strategy or gameplay. And at various stages of the game, it appeared that Minerva may indeed win, but she, too, would leave at least a variety of options for him to reposition himself into a neutral position. He glanced at the board and again stared in disbelief. Minerva was about to lose.

When he looked back up at his opponent, Minerva's attention was trained upon Drake. The man's gaze flickered to the board. Jaw clenched, Drake pinned Minerva with a glare for a few seconds before he dipped his head to whisper in Diana's ear.

Both Diana and Drake examined the chessboard. Diana turned to Drake, and Randal read the woman's lips—*Ye of little faith.*

A flare of hope pumped through his veins. Did Diana want Minerva to win? Randal leaned forward to study the board once more. What possible move did Minerva have? Did Diana know of her sister's terms?

Mentally moving each piece, Randal worked every angle, but with every move, the outcome was the same—he won, which would mean he would be bound to offer for Minerva's hand. He squinted at the wooden pieces, not to maneuver them in his head but to take a moment to contemplate his future. Marriage had been on his list of tasks to accomplish. Love had not been a requirement.

Who would love a man who had seen to the death of hundreds of men? He was referred to as the cold-hearted Beast of Chestwick countless times. So many times, in fact, that he began to refer to himself as such. He led and organized armies, leagues of men into battle, all with one purpose—to kill the enemy. How could a woman love a man who was responsible for such bloodshed? His soul was blackened by his deeds. He wasn't worthy. He wouldn't sentence either of the Malbury ladies to a loveless life. Like all problems he had in the past, he would find a solution—a way to release them both.

DIANA'S MIND REELED as she waited for Randal to make his next move. She squinted at the white and black chess pieces. As far as she could determine, Randal was two moves away from winning. She should feel elation or, at the very least, relief for her sister, yet the ache in her belly had spread to her chest. Minerva would be the Countess of Chestwick.

Drake shifted in his seat and leaned closer to whisper, "Faith has naught to do with this situation. She has forfeited the game—to Chestwick."

"Isn't this the outcome we had *all* wished for? For Minerva to find a gentleman worthy of her hand?" Diana flinched, hearing the biting tone in her voice. She had spoken nothing but the truth. However, she had failed at masking her anger at Drake's glaring failure to declare his true feelings for her sister.

Nostrils flared, Drake crossed his arms and leaned back in his chair. "Three bloody Seasons, and *now* she decides to concede to a man none of us really know."

"At least Minerva shall remain close by." Diana covertly glanced at Randal. Raw power and determination radiated from his tense form. Her heart faltered for a moment.

"Mayhap I should take Chestwick's place on the battlefield."

Diana whipped about to face Drake. "You will get yourself killed!"

Drake shrugged and returned his gaze in the direction of the chessboard, but his eyes remained blank. She wanted to shake Drake by the shoulders. The man was a fool if he believed no one could see how much he cared for Minerva. Diana glared at her brother Kent. Why were men such dullards?

Instead of repositioning his queen, Randal reached for his knight.

Seated on the edge of his chair, Mansville crowded the board. "Opting for the safe defensive play again, Chestwick?"

Randal ignored Mansville's question and set his knight in position, placing Minerva in check. If he had simply moved his queen, it would have garnered the same result. What was the man up to?

Mansville's brow furrowed into a deep frown, replacing his smug smile. Before he could utter a comment, Minerva quickly captured Randal's knight with her pawn. What were they up to? In quick succession, Randal and Minerva utterly changed the pace of the game, moving pieces in a blur so that it was difficult to follow exactly what was occurring.

Earlier, she had frequently felt his gaze upon her, except now his attention was solely focused on the game before him. The ease with which Randal was able to shut out the world—to ignore her—cut deeper than Diana anticipated. She and her sisters shared one fundamental fear—to be bound in a union that resembled their parents. The horror of being married off to a man who neither loved nor respected them, in essence being sentenced to a life with a philanderer and an absent husband like their papa, meant each of them was willing to go to great lengths to avoid marriage. The chess game being enacted out right in front of her was proof.

"It's a draw!" Drake shouted.

Mansville countered, "Impossible!" The man jumped to his feet, his head swiveled toward Minerva, then to Randal, back down to the chessboard, and returned once again to her smiling sister. "Your luck will run out one day."

Kent stood next to Minerva and glared at Mansville. When the man didn't say anything more, Kent took her sister's elbow and said, "Minerva, Diana, Greg, it is time for us to return to Malbury Manor."

Randal continued to ignore her and remained rooted next to Mansville. He never took his eyes off the two unwanted guests. Unable to stand unassisted, Diana elbowed Drake, who gave the silent but observant Cunningham a nod. Leaning on Drake's arm, Diana straightened and hobbled out of the library. The game had ended in a tie. The knots in her stomach should have eased. nstead they only tightened with each step she took toward the front doors. With Randal's silent dismissal of her and her family, Diana was certain none of them would ever be invited back to Chestwick Hall. Diana masked the pain of her ankle, but the discomfort in her chest was hard to ignore.

Chapter Twenty-Two

SEATED BY THE window, Randal waited for the first streaks of morning to appear over the horizon. He hadn't seen nor heard from Diana in a sennight, and with each day, his focus waned. Without the mayhem and ruckus, Randal's headaches had returned as if his mind needed the constant noise. The constant chatter of the Malburys was better than the constant hum of artillery. The numbness he experienced after his mama's death was threatening to once again consume him.

Cartwright entered his chambers. "Me lord. Are ye wantin' a shave this morn?"

Why bother?

No one was coming to visit.

No one was sneaking onto his land.

No one that he desperately needed.

He ran his hand over the three days' growth. Randal preferred the beard that covered a portion of his marred face. "Not today."

His valet bustled about the room laying out some ensemble. "Ye received another invitation from Lord Drake, this time to accompany the men on a hunt, should I decline?"

"No. A good hard ride might be exactly what I need."

"But ye despise chasing down innocent creatures." Cartwright picked up the day outfit and shook his head, mumbling, "Ye needs to be hunting down Lady Diana, not some poor creature."

Hunting for a wife versus a fox hardly seemed an appropriate analogy, yet some might agree that in both cases, a gentleman was out to trap an innocent.

Brushing his wayward thoughts aside, Randal said, "I heard your remarks, Cartwright. I am quite aware of my need of a wife; however, I do not see any reason to simply select the first woman I come across by happenstance."

Standing at the ready with Randal's hunting jacket with shiny brass buttons, Cartwright rolled his eyes heavenward. If the man hadn't saved Randal's life a time or two, he might have considered firing his valet for such insolent behavior. But Cartwright was as loyal as they came, and he'd never toss the man that rode by his side for years.

Randal had walked the perimeter every day, wishing Diana would come dashing across the field as she had a fortnight ago. That one chance encounter turned all his rational plans to dust. He found himself laying in the grass, making out shapes in the clouds, all in the hopes Diana might find him again—an utter waste of time. Time he could have spent on reviewing the estate ledgers.

Randal was not suited to the life of an idle gentleman. He shoved his arm into his coat sleeve. He longed for the simplicity of military life. At least on the battlefield, his days were routine—wake up, fight, and try not to get killed. Predictable.

Randal stood still as Cartwright buttoned his coat.

After a deep sigh, Cartwright said, "I've known ye fer too long, me lordship. Ye needs organized chaos."

Randal's mind caught and mulled over his valet's words—organized chaos. Mayhap his valet was right. But even if he was, it was clear Diana was no longer vested in solving his papa's riddle, let alone interested in him. Her failure to appear was all the evidence he needed.

Randal blinked as Cartwright waved a hand around in a circle and then pointed at Randal from head to toe. "I'm not sure who ye are."

Randal tugged on the hem of his sleeves. "I'm the Earl of Chestwick, and I'm off to join the hunt." He turned and marched toward the door.

"Ye at least look the part," Cartwright mumbled from behind him.

Randal ignored the jab and lengthened his stride, making quick work of making his way through Chestwick Hall. Stepping out into the fresh air, Randal paused and inhaled deeply—he couldn't deny the truth any longer—the structure he came home to reclaim was now too large and too empty without Diana and her family.

A cold chill ran down his spine, accompanied by images of the last time he saw the Malburys. He had believed Diana had understood why he had countered and positioned himself to potentially win and thus agree to marry Minerva. He could have easily decided to win the game, but in the end, he chose to end it in a tie as Minerva had originally established. Each time he had been poised to win, he could feel the warmth of Diana die.

Forcing himself to move, he headed for the stables, attempting to recall what the rules of etiquette dictated for a hunt—to hell with etiquette, he would present himself unannounced as they had shown up on his doorstep. At least he had been invited.

THERE WAS NO need for Diana to look over her shoulder to know who was fast approaching from behind. Isadora wide-eyed, mouthed, "Oh my, what a striking image." Isadora blinked and continued, "It's Lord Chestwick! It is no wonder his enemies turned and fled at the sight of him on the battlefield."

Diana resisted the urge to look. It had taken all her energy to try and banish his image from her mind this past week and had utterly failed. The man haunted her thoughts day and night. Eyes closed, she inhaled, fortifying herself to come face-to-face with the man Kent had assured would not be present at today's hunt.

The beating hooves were slowing, and Isadora closed her gaping mouth to smile. "With Lord Chestwick's arrival, the hunt shall be immensely more entertaining."

"Whatever gave you that impression?"

Isadora ignored her and urged her mount forward to join their brothers and the rest of the hunting party, which consisted of Drake, Cunningham, and a handful of footmen.

She should have stayed at home with Minerva. A shudder rolled through her at the thought of spending another day being questioned by her mama, who was curious and anxious to meet the Beast, especially since both Minerva and she had denounced the *ton*'s claims Randal was ghastly and horrid.

"Are you chilled?" Randal's smooth baritone voice was laced with concern. Concern for her. Being the youngest sister of three and not the babe of the family, not many concerned themselves with Diana's welfare, which she preferred.

Avoiding meeting Randal's gaze, she looked forward and uttered, "Not in the slightest." How she managed to keep her voice neutral and devoid of her inner want to throw herself into his arms once more was beyond her comprehension. She wouldn't be able to avoid him for the entire day. Turning at the waist, Diana was taken aback by Randal's dark scowl. Finding her voice and courage, she asked, "Shall we join the others?"

"Perhaps I should decline and return to Chestwick Hall."

Seated casually upon his steed, Drake approached. "Lord Chestwick! Glad you could join us today." Drake eyed him curiously. "You are joining us, are you not?"

Rarely was Diana torn between two wishes. She cursed herself for wanting the attention of a man who had ignored her for fourteen days straight. Every morn she had held out hope of receiving an invitation to return, even if it was simply to use the library. Every night she went to bed disappointed. She refused to mirror her mama's behavior of staying up each night waiting for her husband to finally pay a moment's notice.

Diana's lips betrayed her, she smiled at Randal.

His brow relaxed as he grinned back at her. "I believe I shall join the hunt after all."

"Grand." Drake skillfully maneuvered his mount back around. "Diana, where is your sister today?"

"Why she's right in front of you."

Drake pinned her with a serious stare. "You know I was referring to Minerva."

"Ah...so you can utter her name without utter disdain. Good to know." Diana urged her mare forward, leaving the two men behind her. "Isadora, shall we ride together?"

Isadora looked back at the men. With pure mischief in her eyes, her sister turned back to face her and said, "Try to keep up with me."

All her siblings were skilled in the saddle, but Isadora was most competitive out of the lot and rode with no mercy. Diana nudged her mare forward to the sounds of the horns blasting and dogs barking.

The hunt was on.

Chapter Twenty-Three

DIANA'S BOLD DEFENSE of Minerva left Randal grinning and his heart bursting with pride. She was a remarkable woman, fierce, intelligent, loyal, all qualities he admired most. Gathering his wits, he urged his mount to join the fray. He stopped next to Drake. "Have you spoken to Lady Minerva since our game of chess?"

Drake straightened in the saddle. "No. Have you?"

"I've not left Chestwick Hall until today." Randal brought his mount to a halt. "Why would you ask if I've spoken to Lady Minerva?"

Drake circled back to face Randal. The man wouldn't meet Randal's gaze, but he did answer. "Because you are courting Minerva."

"Courting!" Randal's hand clenched, causing his mount to prance sidewards. "What gave you that impression?"

Still avoiding eye contact, Drake stroked the neck of his horse. "During the match…there were moments…opportunities in which you placed yourself in position to win… I gathered you ended the game in a stalemate in order to court her properly."

"Ha! You think it was *I* who managed to formulate a way to end the game under Mansville's scrutiny." Randal shook his head and urged his horse forward. "You really are clueless."

He replayed the last ten moves of the game in his mind. He had positioned his knight as a sacrifice, but it was Minerva who initiated the rapid play to disguise her signals. Randal merely followed Minerva's lead. If no one else detected the sleight of hand movements, it was possible Diana had misconstrued his actions.

Drake caught up, and they rode side by side in silence for a few yards.

Noting the worry lines across Drake's brow, Randal said, "Not that you care or have a vested interest, but I will have you know that I have no intention of courting or marrying Lady Minerva Malbury. The woman deserves a man who can love. Love her for not only her beauty but for that extraordinary mind of hers."

"I would wish that be the case for all of Kent's sisters."

Drake's use of the word sister reinforced the theory that the man viewed the Malbury ladies as such. Were all men in love such fools?

His host chuckled, and Randal followed the direction of Drake's gaze. Slightly to the right in front of them, the Malbury ladies skillfully jumped a fallen log and maneuvered through the trees. Both were extremely skilled, but his interest still remained on Diana. Unable to resist the woman's allure, Randal urged his steed forward to catch up to the women.

Drake called out, "They will lead you in the wrong direction."

"Don't all women?"

Drake laughed and replied, "I wish you luck!"

Randal left his host behind and urged his mount into a full gallop. An odd prickling at the back of his neck caused Randal to glance back over his shoulder. With no one about, Drake's easy manner had been shed, and the man rode with determination in the direction of Malbury Manor. Drake may act indifferent, but the man was unquestionably in love with Minerva Malbury.

Refocusing on catching up to the women, he kicked his heels, and his mount obediently increased speed until they were flying through the open field, skirting along the tree line. He caught sight of Diana's hair and marveled at how pleased he was just to be merely close enough to see her. The tension that had grown between his shoulder blades seemed to ease as he closed the distance between them.

Isadora parted from her sister, heading in the general direction Drake had set off for. Diana remained seated in the middle of a paddock, looking up at the sky.

As he approached, Diana turned and said, "Why are you following me?"

Because you have infiltrated your way into my every thought was on the tip of his tongue. Rather than admit the truth, he replied, "I merely wanted to ensure you and Lady Isadora came to no harm."

"You are supposed to be with the others enjoying the hunt." She released the reins and crossed her arms.

He pulled his gaze from her adorable face and glanced about the empty field. "Shall I accompany you to join the others?"

"It took a considerable sum to be rid of my sister." Diana pushed a wayward tress of hair behind her ear. "I wish to be alone if you don't mind."

Tilting his head to block the sunlight from her eyes, he asked, "Is something the matter?"

"No."

She wasn't answering a question with a question, indicating Diana was cross with him. He tried again. "Have I offended you in some way?"

"Offended, he asks." Diana huffed. "You kissed me, and then you nearly got yourself engaged to my sister!" She grabbed the reins and held onto the pommel until her knuckles were white. "I'm not offended. I'm merely confused."

Relief spread through Randal. He appreciated her honesty. In turn, he decided it best to share the concerns that had plagued him all week and had prevented him from seeking an audience with her. "Is it true you shall not entertain the idea of marriage until your two older sisters are happily settled?"

"Who told you that?"

"It matters not who informed me. Have you changed your position regarding marriage?"

"Why is it any concern of yours?"

"It is a known fact I returned from war to fulfill my duties as the earl..."

"And one of those duties is to marry." She nodded and then continued, "You wish to find a woman to fill the position of countess in quick order. Am I your choice to fulfill that *duty*?"

He didn't know how to answer. Did Diana think so little of his affection for her that she would consider herself a mere duty if he asked for her hand?

Diana turned her face away, but Randal caught sight of the single tear that rolled down her cheek.

Chapter Twenty-Four

The back of Diana's riding glove grazed against her cheek. What a fool she had been. She'd thought if she simply confronted Randal and sought out the truth, it would ease the ache in her chest. The ache was now a searing pain. She didn't want to be a man's duty—she wanted love and passion. After days of debate with Minerva, Diana admitted she had wanted to discover the man in the paintings that graced the walls of Chestwick Hall, but now she felt a need to unmask the Earl of Chestwick. Or had the years on the battlefield molded him into the Beast everyone referred to him as?

Diana whistled to draw Isadora's attention but gained the attention of her brothers, also, who were now scowling and had turned their mounts in her direction.

Slowing to a trot to gather her wits, she thrust her chin out and waited for her siblings to descend upon her. "One question at a time, please."

Greg was the first to set upon her but searched behind her instead of glaring at her. "Where have you been, and where is that devil Chestwick?"

"Why are you so upset?"

Isadora answered, "I might have spoken my thoughts out loud…"

"Which were?"

"Umm…that I hoped Chestwick might grant you a kiss or two."

"Isadora Malbury!" Diana groaned. "Are you trying to get Kent killed?"

"No, why would Kent's life be in jeopardy?"

"Chestwick is reported to be one of His Majesty's best marksmen."

Isadora sided her horse closer. "Did Chestwick kiss you? Is there reason for Kent to demand...oh! You have been crying. I'll shoot Chestwick myself for upsetting you."

Before Diana could shush her sister, Kent flanked her on the other side.

"Sister, dear, allow me to escort you home." His dire tone meant there was no arguing or changing his mind.

She wouldn't be forced to marry a man who didn't want to marry her, and she certainly didn't want a man to marry her as a result of a simple misunderstanding or the wild imaginations of others.

She jumped the fence onto the Malbury estate and rode directly to the stables, not looking back to see how far back the others might be. Why hadn't she been wise enough to remain at home with Minerva? On the terrace, she spied both her mama and Minerva sitting with easels in front of them. Diana laughed; it was a close toss-up as to which was worse—stuck painting watercolors or causing a scandal.

Stable hands rushed out at the pounding of horse hooves. Diana slid to the ground without assistance and gave the reins over.

Diana had made it halfway to the terrace before Kent's edict reached her ears. "Diana Malbury, halt right there."

She turned to face her irate brother. "Nothing untoward occurred. There is no need to glare at me."

"No need? You went missing from the hunting party. Alone, with an unmarried gentleman. You know the consequences."

"The entire hunting party comprised of friends and family. I highly doubt either Cunningham or Drake is likely to spread false rumors."

"Very well. But answer this one question before Mama arrives." He settled his hands on his hips. "Have you shared a kiss with

Chestwick?"

Diana's gaze flickered to the left. Her siblings and her mama were about to be within earshot. She leaned forward and answered, "Lord Chestwick and I did not share a kiss today."

"Let me rephrase my question. Have you ever shared a kiss with Chestwick?"

She peered down at her toes and nodded.

"I'm assuming no other witnessed the event."

"You are correct. I shan't be forced into marriage..." Anger rolled through Diana. "Unless you agree to marry the last lady you kissed in private. I believe Lady..."

"That is not the same. Knowing Chestwick has taken liberties with you, I must demand he do the honorable thing."

No longer alone, Minerva wrapped an arm around Diana. "And should Lord Harrow demand the same of you?"

"How do you know of such things?"

"Being sister to a rogue has certain advantages. Ladies rarely hold their tongues and are more than happy to be friends if it means the possibility of sharing your company."

"Bah. You shall not distract me, Minerva."

Her sister did not relent. "Do you love Chestwick, Diana?"

"Of course I do."

"Then I suggest you carefully consider your actions."

Kent turned to Diana. "Why would you allow Chestwick to kiss you if you do not wish to wed the man?"

Diana carefully considered her answer. "It was before I knew he was more akin to our papa than his own."

"What does that mean?"

Diana looked at her sisters. Maybe she could help them all if she voiced their shared wish. "It means I want a husband who will adore and cherish me, not take me for granted."

Kent's brows creased. Diana, flanked by her sisters, headed toward the house, leaving Kent and Gregory to ponder her last statement.

Isadora placed a hand on Diana's elbow. "I know you and Minerva have spent more time with Lord Chestwick than I. And I'd never wish for you to be unhappy. But I am an excellent judge of character, and I don't believe Lord Chestwick shares any of the traits that we wish to avoid."

Diana tilted her head. "How could you possibly know that given the little time you have spent in his presence?"

"Reading people is my skill. I know these things." Isadora hurried ahead.

Diana turned to Minerva. "Don't tell me you agree."

Minerva smiled. "You marrying Lord Chestwick would make me very happy."

"But to marry before you seems wrong."

"Not when you will be marrying the gentleman fate intended for you."

"You have spent too much time with Mama."

Minerva touched the back of her hand to her forehead. "Mayhap. But regardless, Isadora is never wrong about these things. But you have to choose for yourself."

"Choose?"

"Yes, regardless of how things appear, you have the power to choose your future for yourself." Minerva squeezed her hand. "Choose—happiness, Diana."

Did she really have the power to choose? Would choosing Chestwick result in happiness?

Chapter Twenty-Five

THE DEEP RUMBLE of male voices was punctuated with the pounding of booted footsteps carried down the hallway. Only the Malburys were capable of causing such a commotion to his normally tranquil existence. A red-faced Kent stormed into Randal's study, accompanied by a very serious, grim-looking Greg.

Randal stood and buttoned his waistcoat that Cartwright had insisted gentlemen wear even in leisure at home. "Kent. Greg. What brings you to Chestwick Hall?"

Both brothers sank into the chairs on the opposite side of Randal's desk and crossed their arms, and stared at him until he, too, sat. Randal rested his forearms on the wood and clasped his hands together and surveyed his guests' appearance. From their rumpled clothing to the dark circles under their eyes, it appeared as if neither had slept before arriving.

Greg let out a long sigh. "We have come to discuss our sister's future."

Dealing with the Malburys required patience that Randal no longer had. "Which sister would you be referring to—Lady Minerva? Lady Isadora or Lady Diana?"

"Diana, of course." Kent ran his fingers and thumb along his jawline until they met at his chin. "Unless you have also managed to compromise our other sisters—in which case you may choose which one you shall marry."

"Ignore my brother, he hasn't slept. None of us have had sleep in days." Greg unraveled his arms and leaned forward with his elbows settled upon his knees. "We are here to settle the matter of you taking advantage of our sister."

Randal, too, was sleep-deprived. He switched his gaze from Greg to Kent. "Out!"

Neither man flinched nor even moved a muscle to obey his command.

Kent rose and stood behind his chair, placing even more distance between himself and Randal. "Diana confessed that the two of you had shared a kiss…she would neither confirm or deny if you had taken other liberties." Kent's fingers pressed tightly against the wood until the tips went white. "Our sisters claim that it unfair of me to demand you do the honorable thing and offer for Diana if I am incapable of doing the same."

Kent's emphasis on sisters, as in multiple, not in the singular sense, meant nothing was kept secret amongst the Malbury siblings. A weird sensation of longing mixed with anger settled in Randal's heart. How could Diana have shared their private moments with her brothers and sisters? Simultaneously, it would have been rather nice to have someone to confide in or assist with muddling through a week of roiling emotions and volleying thoughts. Randal stood and walked over to the sideboard. He needed a drink. They all needed a drink.

The French brandy he had smuggled home would help. He poured the amber liquid into three tumblers. Picking up the glasses, he offered them to his guests.

Kent met Randal eye-to-eye, and with a nod, accepted the offered beverage. "I find myself in a conundrum. I have no intention of relinquishing my bachelorhood, yet I cannot simply ignore the facts."

Interesting that Kent hadn't simply dismissed his sisters' arguments. Randal's ears rang, picturing the Malbury siblings ensconced in a room debating the issue. He brought his glass to his mouth. Randal didn't regret the kisses he stole. And even after Diana's rejection, he still longed to have her lips against his. Randal lowered his drink and asked, "What are Diana's wishes?"

Greg stared down at his glass. He swirled the liquid around and around. "Our sister did not share with us her preferences." He tilted his glass in Randal's direction. "Do you intend to seek out Diana's hand in marriage?"

"I'll admit, during her stay, there were moments when I could have replied in the affirmative. However, it matters naught what my intentions are. Diana made it abundantly clear that she had no intentions of marrying before either of her sisters and that she had no interest in becoming the next Countess of Chestwick."

"I beg to disagree. Diana has not been herself since leaving Chestwick Hall." Greg frowned into his empty glass. "It is as if Malbury Manor is no longer home to her."

Had Diana been as miserable as he during their time apart?

Randal noted Kent's tumbler remained untouched as his guest paced. "Although Diana remained encamped in the drawing room with Mama and Minerva rather than wandering off."

Greg traded glasses with his brother. "True. She did ignore every opportunity to venture over here, which is highly unusual." Greg sipped rather than gulped down the contents this time. "Leaving a mystery unsolved is rather unlike Diana. Patience is not her strong suit."

"Mayhap she is merely no longer interested," Randal repeated.

Kent mumbled. "To hell with women and their logic." The eldest Malbury ran his hand through his hair before planting his hands on the desk. "I demand you do the honorable thing and propose."

The Malbury lot were rather protective of each other. If he were in Kent's position, he would have done the same. "And if Diana refuses?"

Greg replied, "Then it is your duty to convince her."

"Do you believe I could manage such a feat if her mind is already set?"

"Diana can be reasonable," Kent answered. "We shall return along with the family and join you for supper tonight. Papa and Mama will be delighted you have finally extended a proper invitation."

Emptying his brandy glass, Greg placed it upon the desk. "Welcome to the family."

Knocking back his own drink, Randal leaned back and contemplated the events of the day. He woke up missing Diana, then was crushed by her, and now he couldn't wait to propose. If he married Diana, would his days be as tumultuous or was the discord due to their separation? Randal wouldn't force Diana to marry him. But he needed her.

Randal picked up his quill and pulled a blank parchment forward. Dipped in ink, he ran the quill down the middle. He began listing the advantages and disadvantages of marriage, focusing on devising the list from Diana's perspective.

An hour later, he peered down at the long list of disadvantages. Why did women marry?

Scrunching the parchment into a ball, he tossed it in the air and caught it, then repeated the motion over and over.

The library. He headed for Diana's favorite room, hoping to gain inspiration and the words necessary to persuade her to marry him.

Chapter Twenty-Six

DIANA NERVOUSLY GLANCED at her eldest brother, who was steadily avoiding her gaze by looking out the coach window. If her plan was to be a success, she would have to pretend she was being forced to attend this evening's dinner instead of eagerly waiting for her opportunity to declare her true feelings for Randal. She had chosen to follow her heart. Turning to her left, she was faced with a beaming Isadora. "What are you smiling about?"

"You chose me and not Minerva to accompany you."

She loved Minerva, and never had she ever feared or felt threatened by her eldest, yet when it came to Randal, she felt inadequate, that if given a choice, Randal may in fact choose Minerva. But to confess such crazy notions was unthinkable. "It wasn't a choice. With the possibility of Drake being present, Minerva paid me a whole month's worth of pin money for me to take you instead of her."

Isadora's smile turned into a frown. "I've been meaning to ask you—what do you think she is planning to do with all the funds she's extorted from us for the past three years."

Diana wished she had the courage to pose the question to Minerva directly, but she believed she already knew the answer. "Most likely what you and I both suspect—she plans on running away and never returning."

"If that is her plan, why hasn't she done so already?"

"Because we remain unwed. Minerva wouldn't want to cause a scandal and jeopardize our chances of marriage." Diana clasped her hands tighter in her lap. If Diana was successful and carried out her plan this eve, Minerva would be one step closer to leaving them.

"Ahh...well, even if you do get yourself engaged this eve, Minerva will have a long wait before I marry."

Diana leaned in closer to whisper, "Not if you continue your clandestine visits to the ladies' club in town."

"How did you find out?"

"I may have my nose in a book most of the time while we are in town, but my hearing is exceptional." Diana would have been a hypocrite to criticize Isadora for her escapades. She had made excuses for her sister during the Season, just as Isadora had for her during the summers.

Isadora adjusted her skirts and wiggled about. "Then you well know, it is perfectly safe."

"Safe? You are a member of a gambling consortium. It is rumored you refer to yourselves as the Ladies of Luck." Diana elbowed her sister. "Miss Mathematics here believes in *luck*. I nearly didn't believe it when I found out that you, of all people, were a participant."

Kent's head whipped about. "What are you two whispering about?"

In unison, they replied, "Nothing."

Thankfully the coach rolled to a stop before Kent could quiz them further.

Isadora placed a hand on Diana's arm. "Has it occurred to you that a life with the Beast of Chestwick sounds exactly the type of story you would want to read about?"

Diana gathered up her skirts, ready to descend. "Reading and living are two very different things." She waited for Kent, Greg, and Isadora to exit before stepping down. Their mama and papa were in the coach ahead, and Mama was in awe of the size of the manor in front of her. "What a lovely home you will have, Diana."

Muting her inward groan, Diana pasted a smile on her face and took Kent's offered arm. "I've been an utter fool all my life, believing you actually cared for my welfare."

"It is because I care that we are here this eve."

"I beg to disagree. Marrying me off before Minerva and Isadora is wrong."

"Then you shouldn't have allowed Chestwick to kiss you."

"I was giving the man air."

Ha. She managed to befuddle her eldest brother. It was rather satisfying. Kent slowed his stride. "Air? Explain."

"I found Randal laying prone on the path. I recalled Greg's instructions to place my ear next to the person's mouth to determine if they were breathing, and then the next thing I know, the man's lips were upon mine."

"Sister, mine, from the shade of pink coloring your cheeks, I can tell you are not telling me the whole story."

She opened her mouth, but there was no humor in Kent's gaze.

Moving forward, Kent said, "Regardless of how you feel about the earl, you belong here, at Chestwick Hall."

"I do love its library."

"Then you shall be very happy."

Kent was a scientist like their papa; he focused only on the facts and data.

Behind her parents, Diana mounted the last step leading up to the front door. She mumbled, "At least I'll be within riding distance."

The butler opened the door, and Diana was happy to be greeted with smiles from the staff. Randal, dressed in evening wear, descended the stairs. She almost forgot to breathe.

"Good eve, Lord Wallace, Lady Wallace." Randal turned and greeted them. "Kent, Lady Diana, Greg, Lady Isadora." After performing the perfunctory greeting, Randal said, "I'm famished. Let's adjourn to the dining room."

No teasing glances. No warm smile. Just down to business. Crushed, Diana managed to force her legs to move.

Seated at the table between her papa and Kent, Diana focused on the place setting before her. She had let her imagination give her false hope that Randal would make some grand gesture to reassure her that this evening's dinner was not a forced event.

Her mama's excited voice filled the room, and Diana glanced at Randal. He was smiling and nodding in response to her mama's nattering.

⋙⋘

LADY WALLACE'S CONSTANT and well-devised questions had Randal questioning if the Frog's inquisitions were as effective at extracting information. He found himself divulging information he hadn't believed possible to extract from him by a total stranger. Meanwhile, Lord Wallace remained aloof as if the evening was of no import to him.

Randal resisted the urge to tug at his cravat that he swore Cartwright had tied tighter this eve.

The countess was in the middle of asking yet another prying question when her husband placed his napkin next to his plate and stood. Not once during the entire meal did the man acknowledge his wife. Stepping away from the table, Lord Wallace said, "Chestwick, it is time."

The fork full of braised beef lodged in Randal's throat. Pounding on his chest, Randal swallowed and stood. "Excuse us, ladies."

He glanced down the table at Diana. Her skin was pale and her lips drawn tight. He realized his mistake—he should have attempted to draw her aside and speak to her before speaking with her father. How could he be a master strategist on the battlefield and a blooming idiot when it came to Diana?

He led the Malbury men to the billiards room. Mrs. Humbleworth had made a point earlier to mention that Lord Wallace was partial to playing the game. Entering the room he spent the least amount of time in, Randal gestured for the men to take a seat in front of the fire.

The earl shook his head. "My son has apprised me of the events leading up to this impromptu invitation to supper. I'm not willing to risk the possibility of others discovering my daughter's harridan ways, or I'll not be able to marry off the other two. I shall double Diana's dowry if you agree to marry her as soon as the banns have been read."

The man spoke as if they were entering a business arrangement, not the future of his own daughter. It was not the conversation Randal had anticipated.

Caught off guard, Randal began with the first thought that had his mind awhirl. "Did you just offer to pay me double?"

A grin appeared on the dour man's features. "I had heard of your ruthless stratagems." The earl's gaze flickered to Kent and then back to Randal. "However, no one warned me you were also skilled at negotiations."

"I mean no insult, Lord Wallace, but the size of Diana's dowry is not what I am concerned about."

Kent came to stand by Randal. "Papa, Chestwick is no pauper, nor is he a fortune hunter."

Randal didn't care for the fact Kent had spoken on his behalf. He now felt indebted to the man, and he hated that.

The earl ran a hand over the green felt. "Now that its settled, shall we play a round?"

Randal stared at the man who was to become his father-in-law. The earl exhibited none of the qualities that Randal's papa claimed were essential to be a good husband and father—attentive, compassionate, and committed. He glanced at Greg, who simply shrugged. It was Kent who approached and said, "I want your word you shall honor and care for Diana until your last breath."

Before he could answer, the door swung open, and the ladies entered.

Lord Wallace groaned. "Good gracious, woman, why must you always follow me?"

Lady Wallace's steps faltered at the careless remark. However, she continued into the room with a stiff spine and her chin held high. Diana and Isadora followed close behind.

His future mother-in-law stood before him. "Lord Chestwick, I shall assume my husband has already given you his blessings. I wish to convey my own."

"My thanks, Lady Wallace." He stepped to the side in front of Diana. "A moment, please."

Diana nodded, and she followed him to the corner of the room that afforded them the most privacy.

"Diana, I..." His tongue twisted in his mouth, and for a moment, all he could do was stare down at the crown of the woman he was to marry.

"What were my papa's demands?"

"We are to marry in three weeks after the bans have been read." He bent to search her features that were hard to view with her chin tucked to her chest. Why would she not meet his gaze? "Do you not wish to marry me?"

She finally faced him. He looked into her clear eyes and noted the heightened color in her cheeks. He would be a lucky man to have the fortune to wake up next to her for the rest of his life. Diana's lips were moving, but he hadn't caught a word she said, too busy imagining their wedding night. "My apologies. What did you say?"

Diana placed her hands on her hips and tilted her head. "You asked if I wished to marry you, and I asked if you were merely inquiring as a formality." She raised the back of her hand to his forehead. "Are you well?"

"I do feel a tad warm, and my heart is beating abnormally fast." Her touch had only exacerbated his condition.

She ran her hand down the side of his arm and slid her hand into his. "I would like an answer. Is my agreement to wed you required or merely a formality?"

Convinced Diana would be happier married to him than return to her family, he answered, "Preferred, not required."

"Well, at least you are being honest." Diana withdrew her hand from his and clasped both behind her back. "Frankly, I'm surprised Papa didn't require you to obtain a special license and be done with the matter."

"Is that your wish? To be married within the week?"

Diana raised her face, and Randal caught a flicker of desire in her eyes. She smiled and answered, "Given my future has already been decided by others, I believe my preferences are irrelevant."

It was a test—a test of his patience or of how they were to go on for their future. He matched her position, clasping his own hands behind his back and widened his stance so that they were more closely matched in height, forcing her gaze to meet his. "Your desires shall never be irrelevant to me."

Color flooded her cheeks. "And if I dared to reveal them to you..."

"It will be my honor to make each and every one a reality." Heat radiated through his body as his own desires flooded his thoughts.

"Mama will insist upon returning to London for my trousseau to be compiled and for a dress to be made."

"Is that important to you?"

"Not particularly, but it might be to your advantage." Diana wagged her brows.

The woman was full of wonders. It was his turn to surprise her. "Or we could simply make an adventure out of the event and journey up to Gretna Green..."

"Pffft, that took way more hints than I expected." Diana launched herself at him and wrapped her arms about his neck and kissed him soundly, sealing their future. There was no turning back after such a public display. All those hours worried she wasn't in favor of his suit were for naught.

Diana pulled back and said, "My trunk is ready, and Cartwright assured me he'd have your things prepared, also."

"Managing the staff already? I'm impressed."

Her father stomped across the room. "What in tarnation is going on? Unhand the man, Diana, right this minute."

Diana turned but did not release her hold. "We are off for Gretna Green, Papa."

"Well played, my girl, well played." The countess chuckled and linked her arm through her husband's. "We shall return home. Kent and Gregory will accompany them across the border and see to Diana's safety."

The earl simply shook his head and allowed his wife to escort him away.

Isadora wrapped her arms about Diana. "I wondered if you had a plan. You were far too calm about matters, but I agree with Mama, your execution was perfection."

Randal stood looking down at Diana in awe as half the Malbury clan departed.

Kent's large hand landed in the middle of Randal's back, jarring him from his thoughts. "Shall we set out at first light?"

Diana answered, "I had planned to leave after we break our fast."

"That is a grand idea, sister." Greg gave her a hug. "Congratulations. You shall make a fine Countess of Chestwick." He slung an arm about his brother's shoulders. "Come on, Kent, let's get some rest. We have a long ride ahead of us."

Kent shrugged his brother's arm off. "Ride? One of us should ride in the carriage with those two."

"Good gracious, Kent—you were born ten months to the day after our parents were married. Chestwick and Diana need time to become better acquainted."

Shaking his head, Kent said, "I don't think so."

"Out." Greg gave his older brother a shove. "This is exactly the stubborn behavior that our sisters complain about. Now let's go find our rooms."

When the door clicked closed, Randal scooped up Diana and carried her over to the settee. "I had devised and rehearsed a long speech, all in the hopes of convincing you to marry me. But I find that after your kiss, all I can think about is having your lips upon mine—again."

Chapter Twenty-Seven

SETTLED UPON THE settee and snuggled in Randal's lap, Diana focused on the simple task of breathing. It was no easy feat given her heart was thumping wildly. Randal's fingers began to drum on her thigh. She placed her gloved hand over his. "Care to share your thoughts, my lord."

"If they were not in disarray, I would. However, you have a unique ability to catch me totally unprepared." He flipped his hand over and intertwined his fingers with hers. She mentally cursed the thin material that prevented her from having his skin next to hers.

Diana stared at their joined hands. "For a man who is renowned for the ability to foreshadow others' actions, I can see how my unexpected behavior this evening has left you rather unsettled."

His fingers tightened about hers. She had promised herself to pursue what she wanted. Diana withdrew her hand and removed her gloves. As she slipped her hand back into his, she said, "My hope is that while my actions were surprising, the result is satisfactory."

Randal arched a brow.

She had shocked him again.

Wordlessly, he leaned in to press his lips to hers. She relinquished his hand in favor of running her fingers along the back of his neck. Diana loved the feeling of the strong, warm column against the pads of her fingers. Randal's kisses were slow and languishing. Having a philandering father and a rake for a brother, Diana knew there was more to coupling than kisses. She pulled back and reached between them to slip her hands beneath his coat. "I once overheard Lady Barlington state that had she slept with her husband before her wedding, she would have known what an utter bore he was behind the chamber doors."

Randal ceased nuzzling her neck and stared into her eyes. "Eavesdropping is a terrible habit."

He was attempting to be serious, but his gaze dropped back to her lips as she moistened them with the tip of her tongue. "Do you think it is Lord Barlington's snoring that his wife finds boring?" Lady Barlington had also shared that men respond in like when their partner is an eager participant.

"I don't believe so." Randal captured her mouth. It was evident he didn't wish to pursue the conversation.

Diana returned his kisses with enthusiasm. She tilted her head to grant him access as he trailed his tongue along the edge of her ear. His warm breath heated her blood, but Lady Barlington's comment kept replaying in her mind. "Will you sleep with me tonight?"

Randal leaned his forehead against her shoulder. "Why?"

"To ensure you are not a bore behind chamber doors." Diana wasn't so naive as to believe that Lady Barlington was actually referring to slumber. "I need to know before we wed."

The guttural sound that came from Randal's throat sparked her interest. She clutched at his lawn shirt. "Please."

"My love, you don't know what you are even asking of me."

She leaned back, forcing him to face her. "Do you love me?"

"I do—I love you, Diana Malbury."

"And I love you, Randal Wilson, Earl of Chestwick." Diana cupped his face. "And while I am an innocent, I do have a fair idea of what Lady Barlington was..." Heat flooded her cheeks. *This is what occurs when you demand what you want—awkward conversation and the risk of rejection.*

Randal tightened his hold and, in one swift motion, stood. "Are you certain you wish to find out what it will be like to lay with me every night for the rest of your life?"

"Yes." Diana nodded. "Aren't you a little curious, too?"

Her husband-to-be chuckled. "Mayhap a tad."

THE WOMAN WAS going to send him to the madhouse. Randal laid Diana upon the bed in his chambers and strode back to the door to turn the key in the lock. When he turned back around, Diana had her skirts hiked up mid-calf and was about to drop her slippers onto the floor. He stopped midstride as Diana shimmied one garter and stocking down her thigh, over her shapely calves, and slipped the sheer material from her foot. She held the delicate items over the edge of the bed before they, too, floated to the floor and joined her shoes.

Diana repeated the motion again, drawing her garter and stocking down her leg. Mesmerized, he couldn't move.

She rose to her knees and reached behind her. Seeing her struggle set his feet into motion.

In seconds he had crossed the room and was at her side. "Allow me."

Diana smiled and turned, giving him full access to the three buttons at the back of her gown. He unfastened the first two with ease. By the third, his fingers shook with anticipation. Diana's sleeve fell over her shoulder, and he pressed his lips to the delicate skin. His lips traversed across her back until he came to her other shoulder. She lifted her arms, and he raised her gown over her head. With only a thin muslin shift covering her pert breasts, Randal shucked out of his own clothing down to his lawn shirt.

Her curious eyes raked over him, pausing briefly at his hair-covered legs, then back up to the buttons at his chest. No woman he had ever lain with had seen him naked. Bayonets were sharp and rarely was there a surgeon to stitch him up. Branding was the fastest and most common way to stop from bleeding out. It also left the skin puckered and scarred.

Diana crossed her arms and pulled her shift over her head. Kneeling on the bed before him, she waited. When he reached for her, she leaned back and shook her head. She should be spared from the sight of his deformed body. He released a sigh at the determined set of her chin. Randal kept his gaze on Diana as he reached behind his head and hauled the material over his head by the collar. Instead of backing away, she shuffled closer and wrapped her arms about his waist and pressed her cheek against his chest, where his heart beat erratically.

Diana peered up at him. "I've wanted to feel your skin next to mine from the first time my fingers roamed over your body."

Randal threaded his finger through her hair at the nape of her neck. One by one, he removed the hairpins in her coiffure until her long hair was free and flowed down her back. "And I've wanted to run my fingers through these gorgeous tresses."

She rolled back to kneel on her heels. "Will you allow me to…"

His mind reeled with the multitude of possible ways he could finish her sentence. The one lesson he had learned was that he was no mind reader and the best course of action was to never assume he knew what she wanted. "Tell me what it is you want."

"I want… I want to touch you lying down like the first time we met."

He inhaled deeply.

To remain still and grant her wish would be a test of his will. There would be no hiding his erection beneath his clothing, for he hadn't a stitch on. He'd want to touch her, except he had the distinct impression she wanted to explore his body uninhibited first. He skirted around Diana and rolled to lay on his stomach along the center of the mattress. At least in this position, he wouldn't be entirely exposed.

Eyes closed, he heard a rustle, and then Diana whispered in his ear. "I'll try not to hurt you."

He laughed into the pillow. Weren't those the words he was supposed to utter to her?

Randal's muscles tensed instinctively at the cool soft touch of her hands upon his back. He wasn't expecting her to place weight on her palms nor the feel of her round bottom on his lower back. Turning his head to the side, he said, "Why are you sitting on me?"

"Am I too heavy?"

The inside of her thighs brushed against his sides. "Not at all. I was merely curious."

She walked her hands down his back, then ran them up along his sides and over his shoulders and arms. "Do the scars still cause you pain?" She repeated the soothing pattern.

"No." He rocked his hips side to side to gain a little space now that his cock was engorged.

"Please turn over. I want to see your chest."

Randal inwardly groaned. "I can't."

"Why not?"

"Because you are sitting on me." He jutted his butt out.

Diana's hands came to rest on his backside.

His cock ached pressed into the mattress. Randal said, "My turn."

She didn't argue or press him to view his chest. He felt like an ass for denying her. The pressure of her weight lifted, and then a moment later, she was lying next to him. He rolled onto his side and ran his large hand down her back, and mimicked her movements, running the back of his hand up her side. Her breathing remained even as he trailed his index finger down her arm.

Diana turned to face him. "Would you like for me to roll over?"

"Not yet." He rose onto his elbow and placed a kiss upon her shoulder.

"Hmm…that was nice."

It was all the encouragement he needed. He rolled off the bed and darted to the foot of the mattress. Diana looked over her shoulder at him.

"Do you trust me?" he asked.

She stared at him and nodded.

Randal wrapped a hand around one of her ankles and spread her legs wide enough to accommodate his body. He released her ankle and trailed kissed all the way up the back of her leg. Diana had buried her head in the pillow by the time he had reached the curve of her bottom. He moved to repeat his kisses along the back of her other leg, except this time, he didn't stop as he reached her bottom. Her body tensed.

"Relax, sweet." He ran his tongue along her opening, the salty flavor brought his taste buds to life.

Diana moaned and tried to roll over. When he captured her hips, she looked back at him. "I'm warning you. I'm a quick learner, and whatever you do to me, I intend to do to you."

He knew her well enough to believe she would make good on her word. Randal's cock twitched, and her gaze was drawn to his member. There was no hiding it from her now. He crawled up to lay next to her and rested flat on his back, allowing her full access to view his chest. Eager. She ran her palms over his torso. His nipples puckered, and she giggled.

Randal confessed. "My body is as responsive to your touch as yours is to mine."

Her eyes roamed over his form, especially his cock.

He sucked in a breath as she began to place kisses over his chest. "Wait."

"Do you wish to stop?" she asked, sounding surprised.

"Absolutely not." How did he instruct an innocent to his preferences?

As if Diana were a mind reader, she said, "Tell me what you want. I trust you."

"Place your knees here." He tapped the tops of his shoulders.

Without hesitation, Diana shifted to do as he bid. Recognition immediately flared in her eyes. She leaned forward, settling her hands on the bed next to his waist. Diana was much shorter than he. He lifted his hips, bringing her mouth closer to the tip of his manhood.

He threaded his fingers through her hair. "Take me inside your mouth."

Diana parted her lips, and he lifted his hips. The feel of her lips sliding over his manhood was exquisite. With a little pressure on the back of her head, he urged her to take more of him. He was thick, and he quickly filled her mouth. He lowered his hips and eased out of her mouth. Diana mirrored his movements, lowering her own hips. He reached up to position her over his face and flicked his tongue along her opening. He pressed his tongue to slide between her nether lips. He licked and suckled at the tender flesh at her core until his tongue brushed over the sensitive mound that would bring Diana bliss.

Randal circled her entrance with a finger as he ran his tongue back and forth over her clit.

Diana continued to kiss, lick, and take his cock into her mouth. She got bolder the louder his moans became.

Her thigh muscles were quivering. She was close to experiencing her first climax. Randal pushed his finger deeper. She was tight, but he added another, stretching her. He flicked his tongue faster and Diana shifted lower, the tip of his manhood hitting the back of her throat. He wouldn't be able hold back much longer. He felt the pressure mounting in his balls quickly. He had to regain control. She needed to find her release first.

He withdrew one of his fingers from her center and used it to tease her clit.

Diana moved forward, and before he realized what she was about, she had positioned herself over his manhood. Faced away from him, he ran his palms over her sides and then around to cup her breasts. She was rubbing the tip of him along her slit, occasionally pressing against her sensitive mound.

He needed to be sheathed by her.

Randal stopped fondling her breasts and gripped his manhood in one hand. He positioned himself at her center and jerked his hips forward. She leaned slightly back, and Diana took more of him. He dug his fingers into her hips as she wiggled. Her attempts to accommodate more of him only made him more excited.

"Love, this might hurt a little." Randal guided her hips in a circular motion while simultaneously thrusting his hips further. Diana's breathing quickened, and then she clamped a hand over her mouth as she let out a half-scream, half-moan.

Randal stilled. "Are you in pain?"

Diana shook her head. "No." She began to lift and lower herself. Finding her rhythm, Diana's movements became less jerky and more confident.

His hands made their way back to her breasts, and he pinched her nipples as he found his release. Diana let out a scream that made him smile with deep satisfaction.

Sated, Randal sat up and pulled Diana against his chest. The back of her head rested in the crook of his shoulder. Randal murmured, "Bed sport is exhausting." He held her tight as he lowered them to the bed and onto their sides.

Diana yawned. "It was nothing like what Lady Barlington or any of the Malbury maids have described."

"Shall we do it again tomorrow?" Randal's eyes danced with mischief.

She rewarded him a brilliant smile, though she appeared sleepy. As her eyes finally closed, Diana snuggled deeper against him. "Hmm...I think that is a grand idea."

Randal closed his eyes, too. His dreams were filled with all the possibilities of how to ensure Diana would never have cause to refer to their time behind the Chestwick master chamber door as a dead bore.

Epilogue

TANGLED IN THE bed linens, Diana rolled to stare up at the velvet canopy. She was physically exhausted. Her husband's attentions hadn't waned, even after three months of marriage. Instead of growing tired of her company, he seemed to only demand more of her attention both in and out of bed. They spent every eve in her chambers. And each night, he remained. Diana smiled. Randal never spoke without intention, and last night, he had referred to the bedroom as *'our chambers'* accompanied by a rare lopsided grin.

Merely recalling the incident made her giddy. Every day Diana discovered a little more of Randal's past and the events that shaped his persona. She'd come to realize it may take her a lifetime to fully discover the man she had married. He was like her own personal puzzle.

Randal shifted and raised up on his elbow and nuzzled his nose against her ear. "I have failed."

"How so?" She turned to face the man that had intermittently kept her awake during the night.

"To banish all thoughts from your mind and have you slumber." He pushed back a tendril of hair behind her ear. "What is the matter?"

Randal didn't need to know it was he who preoccupied her thoughts. "I was… I was thinking this shall be the first time I shall not be within a day's ride of my sisters."

He trailed a finger along her jawline and then tipped her face up to his. "Did you wish to accompany them to Lord Avondale's house party?"

"Was that an option? Were we invited?" Her questions brought her husband's lips within an inch of hers.

"No. But if it would make you happy, I shall make arrangements."

She leaned forward and gave her thoughtful husband a kiss. Before he could distract her, she pulled back and asked, "How do you suppose my family received an invite? Drake and Cunningham made no mention of receiving an invitation, and Drake is friends with everyone." As she vocalized the question, the skin on the back of her neck prickled. "Hmm... how would His Grace know any of my siblings?" The bed sheet fell to her waist as she bolted to sit up straight. "Isadora." She scrambled off the bed and donned her robe. Minerva repeatedly scolded her for not logically evaluating situations and coming to hasty conclusions. Diana swiveled on her heel and faced the bed.

Her husband was resting against the headboard. "Did I not share with you that Drake had, in fact, attempted to secure an invite as soon as he learned of your sisters' plans to attend."

Randal's bare chest tempted her to crawl back into bed. She blinked twice to refocus on the topic. "He 'attempted'? Does that mean he was denied?"

"Aye."

"Blast. Then there shall be no one close to protect my sisters."

"Do you really believe they need protection? I made inquiries. Duke Avondale's set are mostly titled gentlemen..."

Diana couldn't resist any longer. She hopped back into bed and straddled her husband, resting her palms on his chest. "Love, you've spent too much time abroad. Those men may hold titles and on occasion be referred to as gentlemen, but they are also all notorious rakes and gamblers, and the Duke of Avondale is their leader."

"Then why on earth would your papa and Kent allow your mama and sisters to attend?"

"Bah, the real question is why would Minerva and Isadora wish to attend? Everyone knows attending a house party only increases your odds of finding yourself betrothed."

Randal's hands ran up along her thighs and came to rest upon her hips. "Mayhap, we have shown them that marriage is not to be avoided at all costs."

Diana could feel his cock twitching between her thighs. She untied the knot at her waist and slipped her robe off her shoulders. "That is one theorem. Do you have others you would like to propose?"

Randal pulled her closer. "Not at this moment." He suckled her breast, and all thoughts of her sisters were banished. They were capable, intelligent women and could take care of themselves.

MINERVA'S TEETH CHATTERED as they continued to venture north to the Duke of Avondale's estate. How Isadora had managed to secure an invitation to the house party, she didn't want to hazard a guess. All she cared about was that she'd be far from Drake, and the man's fear of heights would prevent him from venturing to the Scottish Highlands.

Isadora rubbed her arms and asked, "Do you think I should have secured an invitation for Chestwick and Diana also?"

"Absolutely not. They need time alone."

"Whatever for?"

Minerva's mind raced for an appropriate answer. "They shall be busy attempting to solve Chestwick's papa's riddle."

Her sister pushed her hood back and innocently asked, "Do you think they need our help? Parliament shall be reconvening in a month, and we will all be required to return to London."

"I doubt they need our assistance. Now that Diana is Countess

Chestwick, there is no rush to solve the riddle."

"Why are you contradicting yourself? If they have plenty of time, why not accompany us to Avondale's house party? You are hiding something."

"Don't be silly—what have I got to hide?" Minerva avoided Isadora's gaze.

"Very well then, tell me..." Isadora reached forward and tugged Minerva to sit next to her on the rear-facing coach bench. "Tell me why exactly did *you* pick Avondale's house party to attend."

"If I share with you my reasoning, *you* shall have to explain exactly how it is that the invitation appeared on our slaver."

Isadora's lips thinned into a straight line.

Minerva seized the opportunity to end the conversation. "I gather you are not willing to share...and neither am I."

"Very well, I shan't press for your reasoning." Her sister squeezed Minerva's hands. "Will you at the very least reassure me that you won't run away into the Scottish hills?"

"Did Diana put that fanciful idea in your head?"

Isadora shook her head. "No. I calculated the odds of us returning to Scotland, factoring in the nice sum you have accumulated, and surmised it was the most logical explanation for you to choose to attend Avondale's house party over the others we have been invited to, including Lady Raybourne's or Lord and Lady Moorestone's."

Minerva released her sister's hands and smiled. "You shan't be rid of me any time soon."

"Diana said you wouldn't run away until you saw me settled also, but I won't marry before you do." Isadora pulled her hood back over her head and tucked her arms beneath her cloak.

Her sister was the most stubborn one of all her siblings, but as Diana's choices had proved, love could make one do things never believed possible.

About the Author

Rachel Ann Smith writes steamy historical romances with a twist. Her debut series, Agents of the Home Office, features female protagonists that defy convention.

When Rachel isn't writing, she loves to read and spend time with the family. She is frequently found with her Kindle by the pool during the summer, on the side-lines of the soccer field in the spring and fall or curled up on the couch during the winter months.

She currently lives in Colorado with her extremely understanding husband and their two very supportive children.

Visit Rachel's website for updates on cover reveals and new releases – www.rachelannsmith.com.

You can also stay up to date with Rachel following her on social media.

Facebook: rachelannsmit11
BookBub: bookbub.com/authors/rachel-ann-smith
Amazon: amazon.com/Rachel-Ann-Smith/e/B07THSRH6B
Twitter: @rachelannsmit11
Instagram: instagram.com/rachelannsmithauthor
Goodreads:
goodreads.com/author/show/19301975.Rachel_Ann_Smith

Printed in Great Britain
by Amazon